Dog Days

IN THE

City

Also by Jodi Kendall

The Unlikely Story of a Pig in the City

Dog Days
IN THE
City

Jodi Kendall

HARPER

An Imprint of HarperCollinsPublishers

ISBN 978-0-06-248456-7

Typography by David Curtis
18 19 20 21 22   CG/LSCH 10 9 8 7 6 5 4 3 2 1

First Edition

For Moose,
the greatest dog I've ever known

Dog Days
IN THE
City

Chapter 1

THE MYSTERIOUS BOX

The dog had been in surgery fifteen minutes. I paced the lobby of Eastside Veterinary Clinic, looking for tasks to busy myself with while I waited. It felt like marbles were rolling around in my stomach.

Most of the time Dr. Stern performed routine surgeries, like spaying female cats, but today a dog named Buster was having his ear drained. He had large, floppy ears, and one day he'd shaken his head so hard, it broke a layer of blood vessels in one ear. This wasn't a life-threatening surgery—at least, that's what Daniel, the vet tech, told me—but it was the first time there'd been a big surgery since I started helping out at Eastside.

I loved being at Dr. Stern's neighborhood clinic, learning as much as I could about animals, and most of the time I wasn't alone in the lobby. Surgery Fridays were usually Miss Janice's administrative days. She'd email X-rays to other clinics for second opinions, file blood work results, and return phone calls and emails, but since the summertime was usually pretty quiet with all the family vacations, Dr. Stern had given her the day off today.

Miss Janice was the office manager, and she lived in one of those shiny new buildings downtown. I only knew that because she loved to chat about her building's great "amenities," like an indoor pool where she took water aerobics classes, and the free Wi-Fi, oatmeal raisin cookies, and hot coffee in the building lobby. Sometimes she even took naps on the roof-deck. "What building *amenities* do young people enjoy these days?" she had asked me once while organizing desk papers, and I laughed and told her, "Front stoops—that's pretty much it."

Even though I could have taken the day off, too, I jumped at every chance I could to spend time at Eastside. Mom and Dad had been lecturing me on "not taking my hobby too seriously" lately, but I didn't care. To me, this wasn't just a hobby. Taking care of Hamlet the pig had made me realize that animals were my passion. Besides, now that I wasn't on the gymnastics team anymore, I had more free time to devote to volunteering at the clinic.

Everyone in my family had jobs this summer, and my friends were all busy, too. Tom, my brother and the oldest of us Shilling kids, was home from college and working as a barista at City Beans, a coffee shop downtown. My oldest sister, Ellen, was nursing her wounded ego that she didn't get into a fancy private college by taking an online literature course with Ohio State University. She wanted to get a head start on her college credits before moving into the dorms this fall. Sarah, my next oldest sister, had a part-time job at an ice cream shop, and Amelia, my little sister, was going to soccer day camp. Helping out at the veterinary clinic was *my thing*.

Humming to myself, I opened a plastic flap on the top of the massive lobby aquarium to feed what Lou—Dr. Stern's son and Amelia's best friend—called the "Kingdom." Lou named it that because of the ornamental objects he'd selected to decorate the tank: a medieval-looking castle, a dragon skull, and two hollow logs where the fish liked to hide.

"Good morning!" I said, shaking the small container of flake food until some peppered the surface of the water. A cherry barb swam up first. These were the small reddish fish with a dark strip through the middle. After the barbs, Dalmatian mollies, and rasboras gobbled up the flakes, I retrieved the frozen bloodworms from the minifridge. It was totally creepy handling them, but part of working at a vet's office is dealing with gross stuff, and these freshwater fish species were omnivores. I wrinkled my nose and quickly flicked a few bloodworms into the water tank. "All right, kings and queens of the Kingdom! Enjoy your breakfast of champions!" I said, closing the feeding flap on the top of the aquarium.

Rap, rap!

I spun around. An older man peered through the clinic windows, his knuckles knocking gently on the glass. It was Mr. Takei. I'd known him for years because he lived a few blocks away and always hung out at the community center where Mom worked. Most of the people who brought their animals to this small veterinary clinic were people from the neighborhood. That's what also made it fun. I got to know all my neighbors better, and I learned how to help them keep their pets healthy.

Mr. Takei held up a large, clear plastic bag with yellow liquid inside.

I knew *just* what that was!

I unlocked the front door and retrieved the bag, careful to hold it by the zipped-plastic top so the contents wouldn't spill on me. I scrunched up my nose, trying not to get a whiff of it. *Yuck!* Somehow I'd have to get used to these types of tasks if I wanted to be a veterinarian one day, like Dr. Stern. She tested animal blood, poop, and pee every day—not to mention handling the Kingdom's bloodworms, too!

"Good morning, Mr. Takei!" I said. "How's Cocoa doing?"

Cocoa was the Takei family's little gray pug. He'd been admitted two weeks ago for an upset stomach, and the pH level in his first urine test was abnormally high. I didn't know all the reasons why this was a bad thing, but that's exactly why I wanted to spend more time shadowing Dr. Stern at Eastside. I had so much to learn about working with animals.

"Much better, Josie, thank you," Mr. Takei said, adjusting his eyeglasses. "But we'll see after this test, I suppose. Is your mother working at the community center today?"

"Yep!" I glanced at the clock behind me. "I think her shift starts at eleven or twelve."

"Wonderful. I'll see her there later on. Have a nice day, Josie, and thank you!"

"Happy to help! I'll give Cocoa's sample to Dr. Stern right away. Bye!"

I closed the door and carefully set the urine bag inside a small wire basket where it wouldn't tip over. I scribbled down *Cocoa Takei's Urine Sample* with today's date on a yellow sticky note and attached it to the bag. I pretended to take a picture of it with my fingers—*click, click!*—and imagined what message I'd text to Lucy, my best friend, if I had a cell phone. Lucy loved animals, but she got grossed out by things, too—even more than me! It was hilarious.

I felt my shoulders sag a little as I reached for the broom. At least, it used to be hilarious. Now things were just strange between us.

I'd quit the gymnastics team back in January. Lucy and I had been gymnasts together for*ever*. It's how we met, back in second grade. Even though we went to different schools—I went to public school, and she went to private—the sport had always bonded us. We didn't have that anymore, and I could tell Lucy wasn't happy with me about it. Since I'd left the Level 5 team, it felt like every time I mentioned Dr. Stern or one of the animals I worked with, Lucy would roll her eyes or have some snarky comment. Often she'd zone out texting her private school friends, even though she knew that made me feel left out. Sure, we still hung out with the

Three Stoops crew—what we called our neighborhood friends—but sometimes it was like my sweet best friend was transforming into my snarky fifteen-year-old sister, Sarah.

My gaze shifted to the clock on the wall. Thirty minutes into surgery. The back of my neck tingled, the way it always does when I'm worrying about things. I sighed and went back to keeping myself busy. I restocked the front desk display holders with pamphlets on pet insurance, city bus maps, and pet microchip information. I adjusted all the plastic lobby chairs until they were lined up at perfect angles. I checked on the Kingdom again, and all the fish had gobbled up the remaining bits of food.

A cat meowed loudly from down the hall. "You okay, Storm?" I called out as I leaned the broom and dustpan against the wall of the lobby bathroom. "Be right there."

Just behind the front desk in the lobby was a swinging door. I pushed it open and entered the hallway where we kept the large, wire kennels containing animals we treated and boarded. There were four kennels, two stacked on top of two, tucked away from the main lobby of the clinic but before you reached the surgery door.

I stuck my fingers into one of the top cages, feeling

the giant cat's soft, orange fur against my skin. Normally I wouldn't touch a caged cat; being cooped up and away from their families sometimes made them nervous, so they'd bite or scratch. But I'd known Storm for years, because she belonged to the children's librarian, Ms. Fischer. Sometimes she let Storm roam around the children's zone, where she'd curl up on a reading beanbag in the sunshine. Storm was really friendly with people. But with other cats? Not so much. Storm had gotten into a little "scuffle" with another cat, probably a stray, according to Dr. Stern. We weren't quite sure which cat picked the fight, and the other cat was never found. Ms. Fischer had discovered Storm on her back stoop, meowing and bleeding from her ear, so she brought her in to Eastside. Dr. Stern gave Storm a few stitches—I was lucky enough to be able to watch, and it wasn't gross at all—and Storm's wound was healing nicely. She was also eating and drinking, which was a good indicator that she was feeling better.

"There, there, you're all right," I assured her in a soothing voice. "Why don't you take a little catnap?" I scratched along her neck in the spot that made her purr, being careful not to touch her stitches. But Storm didn't want to lie down in the kennel. She popped up on her paws and circled the cage again, meowing. It wasn't unusual for cats to dislike being kenneled, but something about her behavior definitely seemed off. Storm hadn't been this uneasy all morning. I knew I wasn't a veterinarian or anything, but how she was acting didn't seem to relate to her recovery.

It was like she was . . . nervous.

I felt a jolt down my spine. Animals could sense things humans couldn't. There were loads of reports about wild animals fleeing their homes before an earthquake. We didn't get earthquakes in central Ohio, but we did get tornadoes. What if . . .

BZZZZZZZ!

I nearly jumped out of my skin, then laughed at my silly reaction. It was just the front door buzzer. "Maybe that's Ms. Fischer checking on you on her way to the library!" I said to Storm cheerfully, giving her a final pet along her back. Storm meowed, as if protesting me leaving. "I'll be back in a few minutes."

I swung open the lobby door just in time to see someone rush down the street, wheeling a delivery cart behind him or her. A massive cardboard box rested in the vestibule between the air-conditioned indoors of the clinic and the city streets, completely blocking the clinic entrance. By the size of the box, I guessed that it contained seven or eight bags of dog food. I groaned. Those bags were heavy. I knew from experience! Most of the supply delivery people at least said *hello* and had me sign for receiving the packages and wheeled them into the lobby. It was probably a new employee or college student on summer break who just didn't care about manners.

Even though there were no more appointments scheduled that morning that I knew of, there could be an animal emergency or someone dropping off pet samples, like how Mr. Takei stopped by earlier. The giant box needed to be moved. I cracked my knuckles. I was strong. There was no way I'd disturb Dr. Stern and Daniel in a sterilized operating room because I couldn't handle an unexpected pet food delivery. Somehow I'd figure out a way to push the heavy box inside.

I walked toward the door and realized the usual printed delivery sticker with a shipping bar code stuck on top of the box was missing. There was something else in its place—a regular old envelope. Two words were scribbled on it in messy, hard-to-read handwriting.

My hand touched the vestibule doorknob, and I paused, making out the letters on the envelope.

First, *J.*

Then *O*.

It felt like all the blood drained from my face.

Josie Shilling.

The mysterious giant cardboard box was addressed to *me*—and there were loud scratching noises coming from inside it!

AWW-ROOOOO!

The note could wait. I wasn't about to let animals sit inside a hot box in the summertime! I opened the door and clawed at the wide sticky tape on the box, my heart beating faster with excitement. As the cardboard shifted beneath my trembling hands, the noises inside grew louder and more urgent.

Barks. Yelps. Squeals and howls.

Rip, rip.

I tore off the tape and unfolded the box flaps.

Chapter 2

SEVEN SURPRISES

RUFF!

Inside the box, the cutest tiny black- and brown-colored puppies leaped into the air, yipping loudly. I reached out to pet them. Tiny wet tongues licked my hands and baby claws scratched at my forearms.

"Whoa, whoa there!" I laughed as they wrestled with each other, scrambling for my attention, as if they were just as surprised to see me as I was to discover them.

"Awww! What are you little guys doing here?"

I plucked the envelope off the cardboard box, tearing it open and pulling out the letter tucked inside.

Dear Josie,
You don't know me, but I saw you on the news

a few months ago, back when you had that pig and were trying to find it a home. I found this litter of puppies in a back alley with no mom around. My landlord won't let me keep them any longer, and I'm having trouble finding someone to help. The city shelters are overcrowded. Then I remembered you and that pig. You're good with animals, and someone in the neighborhood told me you help out at the clinic sometimes. I knew I could count on you to find these puppies homes. . . .

Good luck!

I bent down and ruffled a puppy's head. "Poor things, with no mama! You guys sure are adorable. Let's see. How many of you *are* there?"

I tried to count them through the clumsy puppy tumbling, but it wasn't easy. The puppies were mostly black in color, with various tawny- and tan-hued markings on their chests, paws, and faces. As they wrestled, climbed, and jumped, they looked like one big puppy kaleidoscope.

I scratched the back of the nearest puppy. I only knew a few dog breeds, but these puppies looked a bit like Mr. Johnson's old German shepherd, Gruff. He was super smart and and loyal. Mr. Johnson had taught Gruff to run next to him on his evening jogs without a leash, and Gruff always stayed right by his side. Maybe these pups had some German shepherd in them, too. But their fur was a little shorter, reminding me a bit of the black Lab, Buster, who was in surgery today. Maybe they were mixes of both breeds.

One. Two. Three. My eyes darted around the box. *Four. Five. Six. Wait—did I count that one twice?* Puppy Number One tried to climb on top of Three and even got his front paws halfway out of the box. He was strong and fearless for a little pup!

"Oh no, rock climber," I scolded. "You're going to stay right there until I count all your siblings. Hang on, hang on, it'll just be a second. . . ."

I loosely closed the top of the box, and the fluffy puppies started a loud protest of barking and scratching. "Don't worry," I assured them in a calm voice. I learned at Eastside that it wasn't *what* you said to animals that mattered, it was *how* you said it. "I'll let you guys out in a few minutes."

I looked around the vestibule. I needed to get the box inside the clinic, into a safe, enclosed space so I could count them and figure out what to do next. Plus, it was getting really hot in this little space. . . . The pups needed air-conditioning!

I pushed the box inside the clinic with all my strength, inch by inch across the lobby tiles, locking the front door behind me. I didn't want the puppies slipping out while I was counting them!

As I pulled the box across the floor another foot or two, a memory flashed through my mind, making me smile. When Hamlet was a piglet last winter, she'd once leaped over our backyard fence, taking me by complete surprise. She had been so strong and fast! I couldn't underestimate how curious these puppies might be, even if they were tiny.

Once we were secured inside, I moved to the front desk and tapped on the iPad to double-check the online calendar, and I scrolled to today's date. Buster the dog was the only surgery scheduled today, and under "Notes" someone had typed in "office day." Perfect! Sometimes Dr. Stern had back-to-back patient appointments after surgeries, but not today. Probably because she had a lot of prep work for that big conference coming up—I'd overheard her talking to Daniel about it earlier that morning.

"I'm baaaaack!" I said to the puppies, opening up the

top box flaps. The puppies launched themselves into the air, sending me into another fit of giggles.

"Okay," I said. "I need to know how many of you I've got on my hands." I gently grabbed the closest one around the waist and lifted it out of the box. It licked me right on the nose.

"One. A boy," I said, peeking at its underbelly and setting the furry black puppy on the clinic tiles. "I'm going to call you Rocky since you're like a rock climber, always trying to get on top of things." Then I picked up the next one. "Two, boy. . . ." I placed him next to his brother. He reached for my untied shoelace, plopping one paw on top of it and giving it a tug with his teeth. I laughed, pulling the shoelace out of his mouth. "I'll call you Tugger! All right, next . . . Three, girl. . . . Four, boy. . . . Five, girl. . . . Six, girl. . . . Seven, girl. Seven!"

Phew! I was dealing with a lot of puppies. I scrunched up my nose. The rest of them needed good names. Six and Seven looked nearly identical in size and mostly black coloring, but Six had amber-colored patches down her legs, while Seven had a caramel-colored chest and two brown dots above her eyes.

I knew that naming animals was really important for bonding with them. I learned that from Hamlet, the runt piglet my brother had saved from a market farm last Thanksgiving. After Tom had snuck her into his dorm room at college, he ran a contest with his friends about what to name her, and "Hamlet" got the most votes. When Tom brought Hamlet home—surprising us all— Dad said not to call her by name because that would make us get "too attached." But the name stuck, and for two months, Hamlet was our pet pig, fighting for space in our tiny city townhouse. She and I really bonded. I eventually found her a forever home with our elderly neighbor Mrs. Taglioni's brother, Mr. Upton, who lived on a farm outside the city. And I still got to visit her on the second Saturday of every month, too.

The puppies scattered across the office floor, clumsily slipping on the tiles as they ran and wrestled with each other. Number Three zipped beneath the chairs, small and lightning fast, reminding me of my little sister, Amelia. "Well, I gotta call you Speedy with those quick little legs." I smiled, my hands on my hips. "Okay, now what about the rest of you? Hmm."

I turned around just in time to pull Four, a long-legged boy, off a chair by the window. He had his paws up on the glass and was trying to get outside. Good thing it was closed! "You're the little escape artist of the litter, aren't you?" I made a *tsk-tsk* sound of disapproval that I had learned from Mrs. Taglioni. She used to do it all the time at my siblings and me, back before she became our friend. Now I rarely heard her make that sound anymore.

I scrunched up my nose and wiggled it against Four's own little wet puppy nose. He howled and licked my lips, making me laugh and wipe off his slobber. "I'll call you Houdini. But try not to disappear for real, okay?"

I set Houdini down with a pat on his head and turned around just as Five squatted in the corner and peed all over the tiles. *"Noooooo!"* I bolted toward the paper towels on the wall and unraveled a whole wad, placing them down on the puddle and sopping up the mess.

"Geez, did you drink a ton of water this morning? This is more pee than Cocoa's sample! Well . . . my brother would probably name you Tinkle, but I'm not going to do that to you." The puppy barked at me, over and over again, until finally I snapped, "Listen here, Babbles, you need to keep that barking under control, or you're going to interrupt a very important surgery!"

I set Babbles back down and moved to the long wall where we had stacks of "pee pads," big, absorbent cotton mats used for housebreaking pets or for senior dogs who had bladder control issues. The puppies were going to have to go to the bathroom at some point, but I couldn't walk them all—not now, at least! There was too much going on. They needed a potty zone that I could clean up easier.

"Here you go, puppies! Right this way!" I clapped my hands lightly. Houdini romped over, sniffing at the puppy pads, and I rewarded him with a small piece of dog bone from the broken bits we kept in a jar on the desk counter. "Good boy, Houdini! Good boy!" His tail wagged happily as he chewed up his treat.

Number Six pressed her nose to the floor and circled around the lobby, following a scent until she bumped right into the food bags stacked against the wall. Her tail wagged fast, as if she was trying to say *"Look what I found!"*

I laughed again. A dog's sense of smell is its strongest sense. But this curious girl seemed to have her nose pressed to the ground at all times, exploring the clinic lobby like a detective on a trail. "You're like a little sleuth," I said, and a funny thought came to me. When I was little, I was obsessed with this show called *Blue's Clues* about this animated dog who helps discover clues to solve a mystery. I ruffled the puppy's head and said, "Okay, your name's Blue!"

I turned my attention to Number Seven. I couldn't figure her out. She didn't seem to be the leader of the litter, or the strongest, or the weakest. I watched her for a moment and saw how she cocked her head to the side and kept an eye on her brothers and sisters, but the perfect name still wasn't quite coming to me.

I called to her in a high-pitched, excited voice, "Come here, girl! C'mon!" At the sound of my voice, all the puppies bounded across the lobby and jumped on my legs. I sat down and let them leap on me, licking my face and tangling in my hair as I laughed hysterically.

"I wasn't calling *all* of you!" I said as Rocky climbed up onto my shoulder.

Seven puppies! This was going to be a real handful. I pulled the letter from my pocket and reread it, wondering what had happened to the puppies' mother. The owner—if you could call him or her that—obviously tried to keep the puppies healthy and wanted them to find good homes. They looked well fed and they didn't have fleas in their fur.

It felt good that whoever left them here trusted me to

take care of them. But what in the world was I going to do with SEVEN CURIOUS PUPPIES?!

I clapped my hands, and the puppies scattered across the clinic lobby again. Well, I knew one thing: There was *no way* I could bring them home. I'd been through this before, with Hamlet, and I'd barely convinced Mom and Dad to let me keep the pig in our cramped townhouse for two months. And for one little piglet, she'd caused a lot of trouble. I could only imagine what they'd say if I came home with an entire litter of puppies bounding after me!

"Ahhh!" I bolted over to a rascally brown-and-black puppy and unhinged its mouth from a bag of dog food. "Which one are you again? Oh right, Tugger. Looks like I gave you the right name! All right Tugger, you rip it, you pay for it. Those are Miss Janice's rules." I shooed him away in the opposite direction.

Okay. I needed a game plan. I spun around and remembered the wire kennels in the hallway, behind the door. There were only four, and Storm had claimed one of them. The two on the bottom were big crates that the largest animals would occupy, and I knew one of them was reserved for Buster, the black Lab in surgery. I tapped the iPad on the desk again, zooming to the schedule for the week ahead. If Storm continued to heal quickly from her stitches, she'd be gone by tomorrow. Buster didn't have a discharge date. There was a cat coming in for a spaying tomorrow.

Dr. Stern was going to be gone the majority of next week at a veterinary conference. Hmmm. That meant she wouldn't be around to help take care of the puppies. And Miss Janice had told me a million times that her new building did not list "pet-friendly" as one of its many amenities. It was one of the reasons she worked at the veterinary clinic in the first place, because she liked being around animals. That left Daniel. As a veterinary technician, he might have the expertise to care for the puppies' health, but he wasn't fun or lovable. I could count on one hand the number of times I'd seen him smile. The puppies needed someone who would play with them. I sure as heck couldn't hand these snuggly puppies over to him!

No. These puppies needed someone who was more than just responsible. They needed someone who needed them, too.

Someone like me!

Sure, things had been good at home with my family

for a while, when Hamlet lived with us. My dad got an exciting new job; Mom picked up more hours at the community center. My parents seemed happy. Mom said she felt "empowered," and Dad liked the "new challenge." Ellen and Sarah, my older sisters, stopped arguing over silly things, like who wore whose sweater and forgot to return it or left it inside out. My little sister, Amelia, didn't seem as annoying, and my brother, Tom, stopped teasing me about my height.

But after Hamlet left us for Mr. Upton's farm, it was like some magic glue left us, too, and what had felt cozy and safe started to break apart. It happened slowly at first, but our family relationships unraveled by springtime, thread by thread, until we were bickering again like in the old days. Lately, it felt like people wore me out. But animals always filled me up. Even on its busiest days, the clinic felt peaceful to me.

Maybe what my family needed—what *I* really needed—was something to bring us all together again. Seven furry, adorable, lovable things, to be exact.

I felt a huge smile break across my face. Maybe by helping these puppies, I'd help my family, and maybe myself, too.

Besides, it was fate. The puppies literally landed on my doorstep!

So I decided.

I was in charge of these puppies, and nothing could change my mind.

Chapter 3

PUPPY PROBLEMS

The litter of puppies had been under my care for only thirty minutes, and it felt like the busiest half hour of my entire *life*!

First I gave them a giant bowl of fresh water. Instead of calmly lapping at it, the dogs all climbed inside, splashing and jumping around. Water got everywhere! I spent five minutes sopping up the floor and drying off their paws. Rocky and Houdini climbed on top of the plastic waiting room chairs, while Number Seven— she still needed a name!—pushed the swinging door to the back hall, discovering the wire kennel cages there. Seven yelped at Storm, sending the old cat into another meowing frenzy. I scooped the puppy into my arms and must've said, "Shhhhh! SHHHHH!!!" a million times because I didn't want Dr. Stern and Daniel to hear the chaos all the way down the hall in the operating room.

Back in the lobby, one of the brown-and-black puppies peed on my sneaker. I had to run to the hall bathroom sink, soak my shoe, and squeeze out all the extra water. Finally, I scrambled around the lobby with just one shoe on my foot, picked up the puppies one by one, and put them back in the cardboard box. Before I could capture the last puppy, the phone started ringing. I couldn't answer it because Tugger had discovered the garbage can—which I'd forgotten to empty this morning—flipped over the plastic bin, and shredded Daniel's breakfast sandwich wrapper. "Ack, Tugger!" I pulled the bits of paper from his sharp baby teeth, picked up the garbage, and set it on the front desk away from his paws.

Whew! Puppies were cute, but they were also *exhausting.*

By the time I got the phone, I was out of breath, and my heart thumped so wildly, I probably answered it with a voice a few decibels too loud.

"HEL-LO! Thank you for calling Eastside Veterinary Clinic!"

Silence.

"Um—hello?"

Maybe it was the owner of the puppies, checking to see if I got the package? I glanced down at the caller ID. My tense muscles relaxed. It was my house line number.

"Josie? Sorry, I accidently hit the mute button."

"Hi, Mom." I leaned against the front desk of the clinic. "What's up?"

"I was getting worried about you." I imagined Mom's eyebrows pressing together. "I thought you were coming home before I left for work. Everything okay at the clinic?"

I glanced at the cardboard box full of puppies. They'd quieted down a bit, just a few scratching at the box. I peeked into it. Most of them were snuggled up and snoozing in a big puppy pile. I placed a hand over my mouth to suppress a giggle. They were probably wiped out from all the excitement, too. They were so adorable! Airholes had been poked into the cardboard sides of the box, so I carefully folded down the top flaps to help block out the light and noise.

"Yep," I said into the phone, more quietly now. "Everything's great."

Really great, actually!

"Miss Janice with you today?" Loud barking—not from the puppies—echoed in the earpiece of the phone, and the noises got all buzzy, as if Mom had cupped her hand over the mouthpiece. *"Sugar. SUGAR! Hush! SHHHH!!"* After the noise quieted down, Mom cleared her throat and said, "I don't know what's with that dog today. She's been barking at the wall."

"That's weird." I made a face. "Maybe she needs to go outside?"

Mom jingled her keys. "Maybe. Here, Sugar, c'mon!" I heard the squeaky hinges of the back door as Mom let her out into the tiny yard behind our townhouse. "I've got to run to work in a few minutes, and no one else is home—HURRY UP, SUGAR! Do you have your key?"

"Yep." I patted the pocket of my shorts, just to check. "Got it, Mom. Oh—and no, Miss Janice has off today."

I bit my lip, a question waiting on the tip of my tongue. Should I tell Mom about the puppies and ask if I could bring them home? I wasn't sure what she'd say, but I didn't want to hear a *no.* Last Thanksgiving, when my brother unexpectedly brought Hamlet home from college, Mom had been my biggest supporter in keeping the piglet. But we already had Sugar for a dog, and Mom sounded really annoyed with her. I wasn't sure us Shillings could handle adding *seven* more dogs to our family pack.

An idea sprang into my mind. "Okay, Mom. I'll wrap

up here in a few minutes. Have a good day at work. Oh, and Mr. Takei popped over earlier, said he'd see you later at the community center. Bye!" I ended the call and once I heard the dial tone, I quickly punched in Lucy's cell phone number, which I knew by heart.

My best friend picked up the phone right away. "Hello?"

"Hey! It's me."

"Josie!" she said brightly. "Where're you calling from?"

I smiled. It was good to hear her voice sound happy on the phone. These days, I wasn't always sure which Lucy I'd be getting. Best Friend Lucy—or Mad at Me Lucy.

"Vet clinic."

"Oh." Her tone had suddenly changed, but I tried to ignore it. Maybe she was texting, or in the middle of her gymnastics conditioning exercises, or I interrupted her using SyncSong, her favorite new app, where you take a video of yourself lip-syncing to songs. Lucy had gotten really into music this year. She knew all the popular songs and could memorize the words after hearing the lyrics only a few times.

"Listen . . . ," I began mysteriously. "Remember how you always wanted a pet?"

"Yeah?" Her voice perked up. "Duh."

"How about a super-*duper* adorable puppy?"

"TELL ME IT'S AN ENGLISH BULLDOG!"

I laughed. "No, but you won't believe this. . . ." I brought her up to speed on everything that had happened that morning. "So now they're mine, I guess," I continued. "But here's the problem. There's not enough room to keep them here at the clinic, and the note said none of the shelters would take them in. Remember when I went through all of that with Hamlet? These puppies need me—need *us*—to find them good homes."

What I didn't say was that I secretly wanted to keep one. And somehow I needed my parents to come to that conclusion, too.

"Did you talk with Dr. Stern about them yet?" asked Lucy. "Maybe she knows some people who want dogs."

"Not yet. She's still in surgery with Daniel." Even though we were on the phone and I couldn't see her, I could sense Lucy's smile fading into a scowl. She never seemed interested when I talked about my life at the clinic. Or maybe she was jealous that I had other stuff going on in my life besides gymnastics and our friendship. I wasn't sure of her reasons, really. All I knew was that talking about Eastside made things awkward between us, so I rarely brought it up.

It just felt like another brick in the wall between us. Who was I supposed to talk to about all this stuff that was important to me, if not my best friend? Why was I so afraid she wouldn't like me anymore if I did?

"Are you going to bring them home? Seven puppies is kind of a lot. . . ."

I cradled the phone against my ear. "Definitely a lot," I agreed. "No. Not yet, at least. My parents would freak. You saw how they were about Hamlet."

"True. But . . . on the flip side . . . you already have a dog, so you know they're dog people. And they let you keep Hamlet for a while. At least puppies aren't illegal to keep in the city, like pigs! So you're clear there."

"Good point!"

"Annnnnnd, since your parents own the townhouse, it's not like there's a building pet restriction, you know? There's this girl at school who can only have one dog that weighs less than forty pounds. Or maybe fifty pounds. But anyways, it's a rule, and they can't break it."

"You're right. Clear there, too." I grinned. Maybe I was reading too much into things with Lucy. She was actually being more supportive of my puppy problem than I had expected. "So . . . you can have first pick of the litter, if you want. Wait until you see how cute they are."

"I'll ask Mom and Dad, but you know them. They'll say no. Dad's allergies."

"Ugh. Allergies." I sighed. "What am I going to do with all of them?"

Lucy let out a whistle. "I have an idea! What if you brought home a couple, and left a couple at the clinic? Then they'd be more manageable, you know?"

"Hmmm. Maybe. But I'd feel bad splitting them up. They're brothers and sisters, after all, and they're pretty young. And how would I feed and housebreak all of them if they weren't together?"

"Yeah," Lucy said, sounding distracted again. "That would be hard."

I sighed. "I guess I'll think about it. But Luce?"

"Yeah?"

"Please don't tell anyone about the puppies yet. Not even the Three Stoops crew. Okay?"

"Whyyyy? Everyone's going to want to play with them!"

I grinned. I couldn't wait to introduce the puppies to our friends, but it had to be the perfect timing. "I know . . . just not yet. If they find out, my parents are going to find out. I need more time to figure out a plan. Okay? Promise?"

"Yeah, yeah, promise. But Fernanda will be mad if she learns you're keeping stuff from her. She's already annoyed that we haven't been to the pool yet this summer."

"This is different, though—" I stopped midsentence because I heard voices coming from the hallway behind me. My spirits soared. "They're out of surgery! Gotta go, Luce. I'll call you back later!"

Lucy sighed. "It'd be sooooooo much easier if you could text me live updates."

There it was again . . . that hint of annoyance in her voice. "Yeah, totally. . . ." I tried to sound casual. "Hopefully I'll get a cell phone this year. Okay, bye!"

I set down the phone and pushed open the swinging door, zipped past the wire cages in the back hall, and nearly tripped over Daniel as he was placing a large, sleeping dog inside a bottom kennel.

"Ack, sorry Daniel! Sorry, Buster!" I said. "I was excited to hear about surgery, is all."

"Josie! You startled me." Dr. Stern pressed a clipboard against her chest, laughing lightly. "Surgery went an extra few minutes—we cleaned his teeth while Buster was under, too. Isn't it past noon? I was sure you'd gone home by now."

I usually helped out at the clinic on Monday, Wednesday, and Friday mornings, but there was no way I was leaving now, today of all days, when I was in charge of seven abandoned puppies.

"Oh, change of plans!" I said cheerfully without explaining further. Then I made a face. "Why isn't Buster awake?"

"The anesthesia is still wearing off," Dr. Stern said, and my shoulders relaxed. "He'll probably sleep it off for a while."

I gave Storm the cat a scratch behind her ear. With Buster still under and the puppies seemingly fast asleep in the cardboard box in the lobby, it was no wonder she was calm.

"Need anything else from me today?" asked Daniel, closing the cage and standing up.

"That's it, Daniel. I'll be in the office the rest of the afternoon. See you tomorrow?"

I sucked in a nervous breath. If Daniel left now, he'd definitely see the box of puppies in the lobby! *Please don't exit through the lobby please don't exit through—*

"See you tomorrow." Daniel was engrossed in catching up on his cell phone messages, and he disappeared out the back door of the clinic into the alley behind the building. Phew! He didn't even say goodbye to me, which would normally be annoying, but today I couldn't care less. I was too busy thinking about how to break the news to Dr. Stern. I wasn't ready for anyone else, besides Lucy of course, to know about the puppies.

Dr. Stern pressed a little treat through Storm's wire cage. The cat sniffed at it and gently took it with her mouth.

"Sooooooo, Dr. Stern. I have some news. . . ."

She met my eyes. I'd known Dr. Stern a really long time. She'd always been kind and thoughtful, and she was a better listener than pretty much anyone I knew. Her calm energy was one of the reasons I loved being around her. My family was anything *but* calm. But still, I was nervous to tell her about my surprise delivery. What if she wanted to drop off the puppies somewhere, for someone else to deal with? Sure, seven puppies were a lot to handle, but I was born to handle it! I *knew* I could do it. If I could take care of seven, surely Mom and Dad would let me keep just one?

I pressed a palm against the swinging door and exhaled. "I have something to show you." I motioned for Dr. Stern to follow my lead into the clinic lobby. I tiptoed around the side of the front desk, stopping alongside the large cardboard box so it was in full view. I gently lifted the flaps, revealing the adorable contents.

The puppies were snuggled up against each other, fast asleep. It was hard to tell where one puppy ended and another began! I held back a squeal to show Dr. Stern I was mature enough to handle this responsibility.

"Well, I'll be . . . ," Dr. Stern whispered, leaning forward onto her knees. "Where did they come from, Josie?"

I matched her calm tone, not wanting to wake them up either. "Someone dropped them off with a note." I handed her the envelope and watched Dr. Stern's serious expression soften as she read the letter.

"There are seven of them," I said. "Three boys, four girls. I was thinking that maybe they're a Lab and shepherd mix? They seem healthy . . . at least, I think so. I let them explore the lobby and gave them fresh water. But they'll be hungry soon, I bet. I didn't know what to feed them because they're so young. They have tiny, sharp teeth, but I don't know if they can crunch down on dog food yet. Oh, wait." I felt my cheeks warm. "I did give Houdini a little piece of dog bone, as a reward. He came when I called him. Is that okay?"

"Houdini, huh? That's cute." Dr. Stern smiled. She

reached for Tugger, the nearest puppy, and lifted up his lips, sliding her finger across his gums to get a better look at his teeth. Tugger was so tired, he didn't even open his eyes at her gentle touch. "About eight weeks old, I'd say. A dog bone bit is fine, if Houdini gobbled it up."

"I was thinking about the clinic kennels and checked all the animals' release dates on the clipboards," I started, feeling butterflies spring to life in my stomach. "Maybe if the puppies double up in the cages, they could stay here . . . at least temporarily? There are two empty crates we could use." Straightening my posture, I added, "I'd clean out the kennels, of course! You wouldn't have to worry about that."

I made a silent wish while Dr. Stern thought long and hard. She studied her appointment calendar on the front desk iPad for what felt like an eternity. "So, the conference is next week . . . ," she mused. "I'll be gone until Wednesday, and Daniel will be on call. Lou is going to summer camp and then to his grandparents' place. Miss Janice will be running the office while we're gone, but we won't be taking any patients. She has a busy schedule and won't be able to care for the puppies on her own. All emergencies will be forwarded to Downtown Animal Hospital. Let's see. Most of our patients will be picked up by Tuesday. But maybe . . ." Dr. Stern looked at me. "Well. Let's say we're able to board the puppies here for a bit. What do you want to do with them? It's your name on that envelope, after all. Not mine."

I grinned. No one ever asked me my opinion about anything. "I want to keep them here," I said. "Not forever, obviously. But for a few days. I just need some time to convince my parents that they should stay at our place. I want to help train them and get them adopted into good homes."

Dr. Stern handed the letter back to me. "This person trusted you with them, and so do I. You proved yourself with that pig of yours, and I've seen firsthand how responsible you are here at the clinic. You've shown that you respect animals, which is a very important part of working with them. Lots of people *like* animals, but not many truly respect them for their full spectrum of behaviors." I beamed at her praise. "But you'll absolutely need your parents' permission to care for them. Oh, that meowing!" She sighed, glancing behind her. "Poor Storm. She's not used to this much excitement."

Dr. Stern pushed the swinging door to the hallway and kicked the doorstop underneath the door to keep it open. She moved toward the meowing cat in the top wire cage, unhinging the door and lifting Storm into her arms. She stroked her furry head until the cat began to settle and purr. After she calmed down, Dr. Stern gently placed her back into the cage and locked the door. "I have a million things to do in the office right now, and I'll need to get Lou from camp after the clinic closes at five, but I'll be back after dinner for the evening checks. I'll give the puppies a thorough exam then."

Yelp! Rawlf! Arrrr-woooooo!

As if on cue, we could see the puppies leaping up against the cardboard box. We laughed. "Guess naptime's over!" I said.

"Let's move them to the empty cages for now," Dr. Stern suggested. "Buster will still be out for a while."

Together, Dr. Stern and I split up the puppies, securing them in the two unused cages. But as the high-pitched puppy yelps grew louder, so did Storm's meowing.

"Shhh, shhh, everything's fine, Storm," Dr. Stern assured her. Storm began to circle her cage, meowing louder and louder. "I'll move Storm to the crate in my office, where it's a bit less stressful. I don't want these puppies affecting her recovery. She's been doing so well."

I'd forgotten about the travel crate in Dr. Stern's office. That meant there'd be three available kennels now. A few minutes later, the anxious cat was separated from the new loud fur balls in the hall, and Dr. Stern was filling out forms on two new clipboards and attaching them to the occupied kennels.

"Now, Josie," Dr. Stern said, her words measured. "We're admitting other patients later this month for surgery and boarding, and I need to keep two cages open for last-minute scheduling changes. You can keep the puppies here for the weekend, but I'm afraid we can't board them any longer than Sunday evening. At that point, the best-case scenario is for you to foster them at home for the next two weeks while we evaluate their health and temperament and get them up-to-date on vaccinations. Of course, you'll need your parents' permission. . . ." She pulled her cell phone from her pocket, pausing with her finger on the home button. "Would you like me to call them? Perhaps that would make things a little easier."

I shook my head. These puppies were given to me to take care of, and I wanted that responsibility. Part of the job was showing my parents that I was mature enough to handle not only the tasks that went into puppy care, but discussions about them, too.

"That's okay, Dr. Stern," I said. "I promise to talk to my parents about everything by Sunday evening.

Thanks for letting the puppies stay here until then."

"I'm proud of you, Josie." She placed a gentle hand on my shoulder. "You would make a great foster for these puppies. I hope your mom and dad will agree with me."

I tucked my hair behind my ears. I'd heard of fostering animals before, but I wasn't entirely sure what that meant. "What exactly does *fostering* mean?"

"It means you'll be responsible for the puppies on a temporary basis. While I can offer some pro bono veterinary services in the beginning, you would need to buy the dogs' food, keep them warm, clean, and well hydrated, and help train, exercise, and socialize them during this critical stage of life. Ideally, that would only be for two weeks, but it could be three, four, or even five weeks if you have trouble getting them adopted out, so you'll certainly need your parents' approval. Well, let's get these puppies some lunch. What do you say?"

I grinned. "Sounds great!"

For the next ten minutes, Dr. Stern showed me how to moisten high-calorie puppy food with water so it was an oatmeal consistency. Dr. Stern explained that many puppies this age should be eating solid food three to four times a day, and that since we didn't know their weaning and diet history, we needed to minimize their gastric upset. After all the puppies were fed, I carried them over to the puppy pad in the lobby in groups of two, and then spread down clean newspapers in their kennels. Blue loved to sniff at my neck, making me giggle, and Babbles pawed and yipped at one of her siblings who wasn't interested in playing with her. Seven—who still needed a good name—was independent and curious, always perking up her ears to listen and lifting her nose in the air to catch a new scent.

"They sure are cute," Dr. Stern said as I secured them back in the cages. "It's nice to have puppies around the clinic again. It's been a while."

I grinned. "Sure you don't want to adopt one?"

"Ha! Well, I'll need to think about that. But don't say anything to Lou, or I'll never hear the end of it. Now." Dr. Stern smiled again and reached for a file tucked in a hanging wall basket. "I need to take care of some things before the day gets away from me. Are you still planning to visit Hamlet tomorrow?"

I nodded. Visiting Mr. Upton's farm and hanging out with my old pig was my favorite day of the month! "But, um, if you need me to stay back and help with the puppies, I can."

Barely visible wrinkles pinched around the edges of

Dr. Stern's dark eyes. "Don't worry, Josie! I know how important your visits to the farm are to you. I will take care of the puppies tomorrow. But I expect you to take over by Sunday evening as long as your parents give you permission. Are we agreed?"

I nodded, trying to think through how I'd explain fostering the puppies to my family. On one hand, keeping the puppies at our place for two weeks wasn't really that long—it was only fourteen days, and these puppies were so adorable, they just had to adopt out quickly. On the other hand, it took me forty days to find Hamlet a forever home, and even though she was a giant farm pig, there was only one of her.

Now I was dealing with *seven* puppies in a shorter amount of time.

"Yep, Dr. Stern. Agreed. And thanks again." I paused. "But what if . . . my parents say no?"

Her expression softened. "Well, I'd make some calls to colleagues and friends, and see if I can find another foster home or a rescue to take them in. Unfortunately, with my work and travel schedule, I can't take them to my place, even as a short-term solution."

Okay. It was the middle of July. If I didn't find homes for all the puppies by early August, maybe I could somehow split them up between my place and my friends' houses. But Sully had two indoor cats, and Mrs. Taglioni's massive cat, Tootsie, was notoriously feisty, so maybe their places wouldn't be the best fit. Lucy's dad was allergic. But Fernanda and Carlos loved animals. . . . Maybe the twins' parents would let them adopt one? Then I'd be down to six puppies needing homes. With each adoption, taking care of the remaining puppies would get easier and easier, even if they were growing bigger and bigger.

I could totally do this!

"Feel free to spend another few minutes with the puppies," Dr. Stern said as she retreated to her office down the hall. "Make sure you close the front door on your way out."

"Okay, will do!"

About half the puppies were awake. Seven licked my knuckles as I stuck my fingers through the kennel's metal door, and I giggled as Tugger tried to nibble on my pinky. They were so cute and tiny! I racked my brain for anyone else I knew who loved dogs. Maybe Mr. Upton? He had plenty of room on the farm, if he was willing to take another animal. He had mentioned having a dog a long time ago. . . . Maybe he'd want a new one. Didn't some dog breeds help guard livestock? I wasn't quite sure. But dogs loved fresh air. I'm sure any one of these puppies would love to live on Mr. Upton's farm—I mean, I sure would, and Hamlet really loved living there. With its big, cozy red barn, and acres of pastureland to roam, it was like animal paradise!

I exhaled, feeling my tense muscles relax. No matter what happened with the puppies, I knew that my Three Stoops friends, Mrs. Taglioni, Mr. Upton, and Dr. Stern would have my back.

And puppies? If I could handle a pig, I could handle puppies. No problem.

Now it was time for the *real* tricky part. . . .

Getting my family on board.

Chapter 4

THE THREE STOOPS

The following morning, when we got home from a family breakfast at a fast-food restaurant a few blocks away, Sugar was lying by the front door. "Hiya, girl," I said, leaning down and rubbing the soft, golden fur around her neck. "Having a good nap?" Our golden retriever arched backward, brushing her wet nose up against my ankle as if sniffing my skin to discover where we'd been the last hour.

"Sugar's always napping," said Sarah, kicking off her sandals into the hall closet. "She's lazy. Like Tom."

"We're not lazy. Saturdays are meant for sleeping in," said Tom, yawning from the couch. He had stayed behind that morning while we went off to breakfast. "What time is it? Blech . . ."

"Time for you to get up," said Dad, frowning. "Don't you have work in thirty minutes?"

Tom placed a couch pillow over his face and called back, his voice muffled, "FORTY!"

"Welcome to the real world," Mom teased, moving toward the couch, pulling the pillow off Tom's face, and smoothing down his ruffled mess of hair like he was in elementary school and not just home for summer break. "And a lot of people work on Saturdays . . . like me. So hop to it!"

Tom groaned and clasped his hands like he was praying. "Pleeeease make me coffee, Ma?"

"You're a barista," Mom said, laughing. "*And* nineteen. You can make your own coffee."

"Josie, would you walk Sugar, please?" Dad grabbed his house keys from a small wall hook by the door. "I've got to run to the hardware store. Emily, what time are you leaving for work?"

"Twenty minutes or so. Don't forget to get the replacement screen for the back door! Bugs are getting through the holes!" Mom said, disappearing upstairs.

As I reached for Sugar's leash, I caught my reflection in the hall mirror. My brown bedhead was twisted into a tangled ponytail that was coming undone. A swollen spot had formed right in the hollow of my chin. I sighed. Great. Another big zit. Now I'd have to go through Sarah's makeup bag when she wasn't looking. I didn't wear makeup yet every day, but maybe I would start soon.

Ugh.

At least Sully played basketball at the local street courts on Saturday mornings, so I'd be safe from facing him on an embarrassing morning like today. All I had to do was get through this walk with Sugar, and by twelve o'clock, I'd be on a train out to the country with Lucy and Mrs. Taglioni. Sully had been my next-door neighbor for ages, and one of my best friends, too. But back when Hamlet entered our lives, I started to realize I had a crush on him. Lucy said he had a crush on me, too. She said he even *told* her that! But then he started acting awkward around me.

Sully wanted to be a detective when he grew up, and he was always investigating different cases and writing theories in a notebook. He used to talk about them all the time. Sometimes he'd even ask to go to the library with me, or we'd circle our favorite newspaper headlines on his front stoop. But lately, instead of sharing things with me, Sully just dribbled his basketball, up and down, up and down, like he was trying to dribble out our friend-ship, too.

But I still liked him. And I didn't know what to think about that, either.

In the mirror, I saw a pink streak creep up my neck just thinking about Sully. I quickly unraveled my hair mess so my siblings wouldn't notice and tease me. *Why* did I have to blush so easily? It was a curse!

Our golden retriever whined at the door. "Sorry, Sugar," I said. "Thanks A LOT for helping, guys," I snapped at my siblings, who were just lounging around doing nothing. I only had an hour before my train! "She's your dog, too, you know."

Amelia ruffled Sugar's head. "And she's the cutest oldest dog on the planet! Yes, she is! Yes, she is!"

Sugar's tongue flopped out of her mouth. She loved it when Amelia talked to her in a baby voice.

"Not the oldest dog on the planet," said Ellen. Her dangly dragon earrings shook as she turned her head from the television toward us. "Some dogs can live to fifteen, even sixteen years of age."

"Whoa. That's how old Sarah's is!" said Amelia.

"Well, technically it's much older. Dogs don't age the way people do, Millie," continued Ellen. "Some say that every one year of a human's life is equivalent to seven years for a dog."

"It's called dog years," I added.

"So Sugar is . . ." Amelia ticked off the multiplication equation on her finger. "A hundred years old?"

"Exactly," said Tom, who had still barely moved from the couch, especially now that Ellen was flipping through the television channels.

"It's EIGHTY-FOUR," I corrected them both, smirking at my brother.

"So, I rounded up." Tom shrugged. "Tomato, tomah-to."

"Aw! She's even older than Grandma!" Amelia squealed.

Sarah glanced up from her cell phone. Now that she was almost sixteen and had agreed to help pay for it with her summer paychecks, Mom and Dad said she could have one and added her to their phone plan. I wanted a cell phone, too, but Sarah's sure was annoying, always lighting up with notifications and practically attached to her hand at all times. She was on that music app, too, SyncSong, the one Lucy and Fernanda were so obsessed with.

Sarah fired off another text message. She was getting

super fast at typing with her thumbs. I scowled. Not that I was jealous or anything.

"Word to the wise, Josie," she said, glancing up for a brief moment as I started to walk out the door. "You might want to change your shirt before walking the dog. You've got, like, pit stains."

Tom burst into obnoxious hysterics and threw Sarah an air high five. She rolled her eyes instead of raising her palm to high-five back. Sometimes my brother's sense of humor drove us all up the wall.

"Whoa, whoa, JoJo!" Tom pinched his nose. "I thought I recognized the smell of BO."

"You're so immature. I do *not* smell like BO." My face burned hot. I wanted to melt into the floorboards.

"JoJo! BO! JoJo BO!" my brother chanted.

"Stop it!"

"Tom, Sarah, you're both so rude," Ellen broke in, pressing pause on the remote. "Don't make fun of Josie like that. It's perfectly natural and healthy to sweat. That's how humans cool down." Then she glanced at me and added gently, "But, Josie, maybe you should give that shirt to Millie—isn't it a little small on you now?" She clucked her tongue in disapproval and pressed the play button on the television remote. The headline news

51

resumed. Ugh! So much for having cable television in the house. I hardly ever wanted to be in the living room with my family these days!

"You're all *so* annoying. And when do you go back to college again?" I said to Tom, bolting out the front door as he bellowed behind me, *"Smell ya later!"*

I let the screen door slam loudly behind the dog and me. I drew in a deep breath of the hot morning air, staring at the cars whizzing down the street. My skin felt like it was on fire, and it wasn't from the bright sunshine. I hated it when my siblings piled up on me like that.

"C'mon, Sugar." I petted her on the head and instantly felt a little better. As much as I didn't want to walk her in the summer heat right now, having some time away from my family sounded fine by me. A walk could do us both some good.

Sugar padded gingerly down the steps of our front stoop until she found a place to go to the bathroom in a patch of grass by a streetlamp. She was a slow walker these days. She sniffed at the hedges as we strolled down the sidewalk, past the Three Stoops, which was what we called the trio of front steps where our crew of friends hung out. Carlos and Fernanda, Sully, and I all lived right next to each other, and our city townhouses all had matching brick front stoops. Thank goodness none of my friends were outside right now, so they didn't see me in my pit-stained, sweaty glory.

Sugar and I rounded the corner across from the library. We meandered a few more blocks. Suddenly she turned around, tugging me hard in the opposite direction. "This way, girl," I said, pulling her back. "This is the route we always take." She circled her body again, sniffing at a street sign, and then lifted her nose in the air, making me laugh at her confusion. I gave her head a *pat-pat*. "Don't worry, we're not lost! We walk here every day!"

Sugar's panting went from slow, heavy breaths to short, quick ones. I started to worry. Then she peed again, even though she already went to the bathroom a block or two ago. Finally she lay down in the middle of the sidewalk, beneath the shade of a maple tree with big, leafy branches. Maybe she was just hot?

I tucked my fingers between her fur and brown leather collar to scratch right on the neck, one of her favorite spots. I smiled, running my hand along the worn leather. It was the collar she'd had for years and years, molded like a favorite old belt, with identification tags that were once painted bright blue but had chipped and faded to a softer, quieter blue over time. Just like Sugar's personality.

I felt worry tug at my heart. "Oh, Sugar, I know it's hot out. I'm sorry. I shouldn't have walked you so far. I was just so mad at Tom and Sarah and . . . okay, take a little rest. We'll head home in a few minutes." Her eyes drooped closed. I sat down on the sidewalk next to her and wrapped my arms around her neck, letting myself melt into her cozy fur. "I love you, Sugar," I whispered into her floppy ear. She was hard of hearing these days, but her ears twitched a little, so it felt like she heard me.

Besides, even if she didn't, animals can feel love, too. They can sense it.

"Uh—Josie? You okay?"

I froze. I knew that voice as well as I knew my brother's and sisters' voices, my best friend's voice, even my parents'—

After all, he'd been my next-door neighbor for as long as I could remember.

I took a breath and dropped my arms from around Sugar's neck to the sidewalk. A flush crept across my cheeks as I turned to meet his eyes. He stood a few feet away, his hands in his pockets, baseball hat turned sideways and backpack hanging off one shoulder.

Sully.

I stood up quickly. "Oh! Hey, Sully," I said, trying to sound casual, even though I was mortified inside that we'd bumped into each other when I looked like a disaster.

"Why're you lying down on the sidewalk? Is your dog hurt?"

"Sugar? No, I think she's fine. Just took a rest is all." I gave her leash an encouraging tug, and she rolled back onto her feet. Hallelujah! Sugar was giving me an out, and I was going to take it. "Anyway, we gotta go. Lucy and I are going to see Hamlet in a bit."

"Oh, yeah! How's Hamlet doing?"

I broke into a grin. "Great! She's *so* big now and seems really happy on the farm. She likes the mud, grass, and cedar chips more than the cave we made her under the stairs, to be honest. And Mr. Upton put a baby pool in her pen. Sometimes she just lies in it for hours! You know, like, um, bathing."

Why. Was. I. Rambling?!

"That's cool. . . ."

Usually boys didn't make me nervous. I mean, I talked to Carlos practically every day this summer. But there was something about the way Sully looked at me and his shy smile that made my heart beat a little faster than normal.

Sully shuffled his sneakers. I cleared my throat. An eternity passed. All I could think about was my sweat and zit and probably-too-small shirt and whether or not Sully noticed those things, too.

"I should, um, take Sugar back," I said finally.

"Okay. Sure." He didn't meet my eyes. "I'll—um—walk with you."

"Okay."

"I was going that way anyway," he added quickly.

"Right." I shrugged like I didn't care, even though I absolutely, totally cared.

Normally walking next to Sully would make my skin tingle, but right now all I felt was embarrassed.

I tried to position Sugar to walk between us—*did I really smell like BO?!*—but it wasn't working. Ellen had trained Sugar to walk on the left side of her handler, the way all the dog professionals do, apparently, and me tugging her to my right side had her all confused. She kept cutting me off, or looping the leash behind me, trying to get back to the side she was used to.

"How's your, uh, July going?" Sully asked. "Haven't seen you since the fireworks. Not that I was looking. Um, you know what I mean. Like on the stoops and stuff."

I felt my cheeks redden. So was he looking for me or not? I'd known Sully all my life, and he'd always made perfect sense to me until last winter. Would things *ever* be normal between us again, when we could just chat and hang out like no big deal?

"Why, have you called a meeting or something?" My tone came out sharper than I meant it to. Usually our group of friends looped a pink bike chain around Sully's front stoop, which was the official way our friends called a Three Stoops meeting. It started when we were little kids, but nowadays most of my friends just texted each other, so it was more symbolic than anything else. I felt myself start to panic, the way I did when I felt my friendship with Lucy slipping away. Had the Three Stoops been holding meetings without me this summer?

"No, um, *I* haven't, I mean?"

That wasn't really an answer. Was he saying that he hadn't called a meeting, but one of our other friends had and hadn't invited me? I frowned. "I've just been spending a lot of time at Eastside," I explained, as if that would make me feel better.

Should I tell him about the puppies? I trusted Sully, but I wasn't sure if I was ready to confide in him. I bit my lip. No, not yet. If he told his sister Trish, she'd definitely text my sister Sarah, and I needed to talk to my parents first. Word travels fast in the neighborhood, and I had to play my cards just right.

I eyed the spiral notebook tucked underneath his arm. "Are you working on a new case?"

Sully's eyes widened, and he reached for his spiral-bound notebook. A look of relief washed over his face as he realized it was closed.

"You are, aren't you?"

Sully always kept a notebook with him. He wanted to be a detective. Over the holidays, he'd helped me solve Operation Home for Hamlet, and the whole Three Stoops gang had helped build buzz around the pig by creating a website, handing out fliers, having our friends and family share on social media, and making phone calls. I couldn't have found Hamlet a forever home without them! But this was the first time I suspected a new Case File was open, and it felt like a betrayal no one had told me about it yet. "You haven't called a Three Stoops meeting about this. . . ." I eyed him suspiciously.

"No, not yet. Hopefully soon?" Sully mumbled. "But I'm waiting on some key intel from an eyewitness."

Of course Sully would use words like *intel* and

eyewitness. But something about this felt weird. We always worked on cases together. What would make this one any different? First I was losing Lucy, and now it felt like I was losing Sully, too.

We crossed the street in awkward silence. I spotted Lucy waiting for me up ahead. It looked like she and the twins were drawing with sidewalk chalk, and Lucy was tugging them into a selfie photo. I could hear the guitar of a song blaring from Lucy's phone speaker, even from down the street.

"Hey!" Sully called out to them, and Fernanda's hand shot into the air, waving.

"Hey, guys, hey, Sugar!" Lucy squealed, running over to my dog and ruffling her fur. "Awwww, her face looks so white and gray in the sunlight."

A pang of sadness burst inside my heart. I didn't like being reminded that she was looking old. I couldn't imagine life without good old Sugar around!

"She had to rest a few blocks away. Too hot for her today."

"Aw," said Lucy. "You can rest here with us, Sugar."

"What're you guys doing here?" I asked. I was only supposed to meet up with Lucy today. It's not that I wasn't happy to see the rest of our friends, but after

Sully's mysterious reaction with his notebook, I wasn't sure if they'd been holding meetings behind my back when I was at the clinic or something.

"Amelia left her sidewalk chalk out," Carlos said, not looking up from his drawing. "We're making a big picture." For as long as I'd known him, Carlos had been interested in art. He was naturally talented and getting even better, now that he was taking regular drawing and painting classes at the community center where my mom worked. A lot of the time during our meetings, he sketched with charcoal pencils in a drawing notebook, so it was cool to see him create something different, and something pretty that was for the whole neighborhood to look at.

"We're heading to the pool in like five," added Fernanda. Her family had a YMCA membership, and she and Carlos spent a lot of time with their swim team friends during summertime. Fernanda tapped her sandal on the cement and popped her gum. "Waiting on Mom now. She's always late. We should just take the bus, Los. This is getting ridiculous!"

"I think I'm going to stay and finish this," Carlos said, narrowing his eyes and studying the drawing.

"You can't just *stay*. We have practice!"

"Eh, I guess." Carlos didn't look up, so he missed Fernanda rolling her eyes. I tried not to laugh. They were the only twins I knew, and they had totally different personalities. Fernanda liked a busy schedule, even during the summer, because she was always coding or swimming. Carlos was much more go with the flow, which drove his sister bonkers.

"You're going to miss swimming for sidewalk chalk?" Fernanda said, dusting the pigment off her fingers. "This stuff is for babies."

"I'm an artist. I work with all media," he said casually. "And you weren't complaining a minute ago when I let you color pink hair on that girl." He pointed at one of the drawings, and it reminded him of something. He changed the subject. "Hey, Lucy, you still owe me a photo of the Hamlet sign hanging in the barn."

In Carlos's spring art class at the community center, he'd painted Hamlet's name on a piece of driftwood, and we'd taken it to the farm to nail above her pen.

Lucy snapped her fingers. "That's right! I totally forgot last month. I'll take a pic today. It's like your barn gallery! Aw, you guys totally need to come to the farm sometime. You sure you can't come today?"

"Hello, SWIMMING?!" Fernanda sighed as if no one

listened to her. She stood up, dusted off her hands again, and yelled up to an open window, "MOM! COME *ON*!"

"Mom's in the shower. She can't hear you, no matter how loud you yell for her," said Carlos. "Just go inside."

Fernanda blew a bubble with her gum and popped it with her teeth.

"I definitely want to see Hamlet," said Carlos. "Maybe later this summer."

Lucy straightened her posture, lifting up onto her toes and squeezing her calves, always so graceful as she lowered down to her heels. I bit my lip, remembering all the times I'd spent conditioning and practicing my gymnastics skills throughout the day, too. Sometimes I still caught myself doing things like that. Movements like calf stretches and lunges and twirls were once my habits, too.

You're doing the right thing, I reminded myself about gymnastics. I didn't have time to both do competitive gymnastics and help out at the veterinary clinic. After taking care of Hamlet, I knew that being with animals was what I really wanted to do and gymnastics was just a hobby. I was good at the sport, but I wasn't *amazing* like Lucy. And that was okay. I was amazing at other things. I stood a little taller. I was doing the right thing.

At least, I was pretty sure I was.

I glanced at Sully. He dribbled his basketball on the sidewalk. He'd pretty much stopped talking to me as soon as we were with our friends. Not that Sully was a big talker, but still. He was off to the side, doing his own thing.

I felt my face flush again with heat. Maybe he liked me a few months ago, but something must've changed this spring, because there was no way he liked me now.

I looked back at Carlos's drawing, trying to command my body to stop sweating from the heat and my out-of-control nerves. It was *embarrassing*. Maybe Sully only wanted to be friends, not my boyfriend. But I couldn't help it. He'd been my neighbor forever, but I couldn't just melt away this crush I had on him.

Carlos looked up, smiling. "A barn gallery," he said, and an image of his painted Hamlet sign appeared in my mind again. "I like that. Maybe I'll make signs for the rest of the animals. What else is on the farm again, that has a stall or whatever? Horses?"

"Yep! Three horses, a new donkey, some chickens . . ." Lucy ticked the animals off on her fingers.

For the first time I really took in what Carlos was drawing on the sidewalk. It wasn't just some random sketch. This was a colorful picture of children's faces—black, white, brown, yellow, green, and gold—filling up an entire concrete square along the sidewalk in front of the Three Stoops.

"Wow," I breathed. "I just walked by here like thirty minutes ago. How did you draw this so fast?"

Carlos shrugged. "Just practice, I guess. I'm working on perspective and shading."

Lucy held up the yellow chalk. "I got to help with the sun," she said proudly, pointing the chalk down like an arrow. I laughed. Lucy met my eyes, and I watched her expression shift to alarm. She mouthed, *ARMPITS!* and I snuck a peek down at my shirt.

Ack! There were two big wet marks underneath my arms. I wanted to sink into the cement, but instead I mouthed back, *THANK YOU!*

I had to get out of here!

I tugged Sugar toward our front steps. "Gotta give Sugar water and change before we leave. . . . BRB!"

I bolted into my house—well, as fast as you can bolt with a tired twelve-year-old golden retriever—before anyone said anything else to me. I held Sugar's long, bushy tail so it didn't get caught in the door as it closed behind us.

Phew!

"Josie, is that you?" Dad's voice carried from the dining room.

"Yeah, Dad! Double-check Sugar's got water, okay?" I unclipped her leash and she retreated into the kitchen.

"Mrs. Taglioni called. Twenty minutes until you need to leave for the train! She'll meet you out front. Did Mom give you money for your ticket?"

"Yep, Dad, and thanks!"

There was hardly any time to get changed! I raced up the steps into the bedroom that I shared with Amelia and Sarah. Ellen had moved out of the girls' room and into the basement last year, after Tom moved away to college, and since the only other bedroom we had was my parents' room, Tom was crashing on the couch and at his friends' houses all summer long while he worked at City Beans.

Thankfully, no one was in our room. I tore through my open dresser drawers. I hadn't done laundry in ages. My family was always hogging the washer and dryer. I pulled out shirts and shorts. *Too small, too big, too short.* Finally, I found a ratty pair of jean shorts that still fit and an old Hard Rock Cafe Chicago hand-me-down shirt that was at least clean and unstained. I changed in a flash and, right before I zipped back outside, threw on a sticky layer of the half-melted deodorant that was still at the bottom of my old gymnastics bag. Then I dabbed a little of Sarah's concealer over my chin pimple, even though her skin is a little darker than mine. I looked in the mirror, sighing. It covered up some of the redness, even though the concealer wasn't a great match with my skin color. But I didn't have time to worry about that now.

Back outside, Sully was trying to spin the basketball on his finger. Fernanda was talking about a tricky new code she was working on, and how her swimming friends were always gossiping about each other. "And Mom's never on time with anything," she grumbled. "She's giving me so much anxiety!"

"Your overscheduled summer is what's giving you anxiety," said Carlos, holding up a hand to block his face from the bright sunlight.

"Whatever." Fernanda looked up at the open upstairs window again. "MOMMM!"

"She still . . . can't . . . hear . . . you!" singsonged Carlos.

"Hey, Sully," said Lucy. "Do you have your notebook handy? I have a new case to add to it."

"Yeah?" Sully stopped dribbling, but his eyes flicked to me. It was almost as if he didn't want to open the notebook.

"Yep! It's a good one. About Josie."

Sully's cheeks flushed pink, and I snapped my head toward Lucy. "Uh, you *do* know I'm standing here, right?"

She threw me a sly grin. Uh-oh. Lucy wouldn't blab about the puppies after I told her not to, would she? Then I had an even more panicked thought. Could she possibly say something about my crush on Sully?!

Nooooo, I mouthed, but Lucy just smiled and pressed her shoulders back.

"I've named it the Case for Getting Josie Back on the Gymnastics Team."

"Oh geez. That again?" Fernanda scowled. "Josie's like, really into veterinary camp. No offense, Josie."

"Veterinary camp," I repeated with a laugh. It was sort of a funny nickname for Eastside, but something about Fernanda's tone made me feel like there was a hidden jab somewhere. Was she annoyed with me working at the clinic, like Lucy? I wasn't gone that often . . . was I? Besides. They were super busy, too! It wasn't as if my friends were just hanging around the Three Stoops without me.

Were they?

I glanced at my watch, wondering when Mrs. Taglioni was going to come outside. "Lucy, it's almost time to go. I don't think we can—"

"Introducing, Exhibit A!" Lucy broke in.

I widened my eyes. "You have evidence?"

Lucy held her cell phone high in the air. Oh no. Once all our friends were paying attention, she tapped on a few icons and suddenly a sharp but jerky video began to play on the screen.

"Next up, Josie Shilling for Team Universal, on the uneven bars!" said a loud, buzzy voice radiating from a speaker.

And there I was, standing in my glittery long-sleeved competition leotard in front of the uneven bars, clapping my hands together and sending a cloud of chalk into the air. I felt my mouth go dry. I remembered this moment like it was yesterday. I would never, ever forget it.

And yet, I'd never seen a video of the performance. My eyes were glued to the screen. Lucy's mom must've filmed it from the stands, I figured. Watching it now was like seeing a stranger on YouTube, because I felt so different from that person competing all those months ago. In the video, I pressed my shoulders back and lifted my chin high. And then I pounced on the springboard, hands snatching the lower bar and legs glide kipping to the bar.

I barely breathed as I watched my routine unfold, remembering how tight the new grips had felt on my fingers and palms, but that they felt like armor, too, protecting me, making me feel bold. I remembered how surprised I'd been when Sarah had spent her own money to buy them for me, and how she'd sneaked up on me at the gymnastics meet just to surprise me. My eyes welled with tears. How was that the *same* sister who teased me in front of my siblings just an hour ago? Who was so preoccupied with her friends and her phone that she couldn't care less about me?

My eyes stayed locked on Lucy's phone screen. I watched as I swung around the high bar, muscles tight and body linear, my ponytail flipping ahead of my body. The high bar gently gave in the middle during each rotation and turn, and I could faintly hear soft cheers in the distant bleachers: *"C'mon, Josie! You can do it!"*

I felt my heart begin to race, anticipating what was next. The flyaway dismount. I swung back and forth, back and forth, and kept my body long and tight as I released the bar.

I heard Coach's cue loud and clear in my head now, just as I had then.

Look for the mat!

My feet landed hard on the plastic mat. I stuck the landing, and the crowd erupted in cheers. I looked like a little doll, raising her arms high and saluting the judges' table, before marching off the mat and crumpling into a hug with Lucy.

I almost crumpled into tears just watching it.

"Wow," said a voice on camera, and I realized that Lucy's parents had been sitting near mine, because that was my Mom's voice. "She was incredible!"

My stomach fluttered. She rarely sounded proud of me for anything these days. She was always so busy, it didn't feel like she had much time for me, let alone interest in what I was up to. The only reason she called me at Eastside yesterday was because she was worried I wasn't home yet, not because she wanted to know about Buster's surgery.

I sighed as Lucy tapped the stop button on the video clip. "See?" she said. "SUPER-strong evidence."

I swallowed hard, trying to process what I was feeling in that moment. Why was my chest tightening up? Because I missed being on the gymnastics team, because I saw my mom emotional over my victory, or because my friendship with Lucy once felt so much easier? I wasn't sure. It felt good to relive a moment so important to me. But I also felt confused inside.

Sad, almost.

I frowned. "No case. And no evidence." I waved my hands toward the whole crew. "Everyone here has seen me compete already. This isn't anything new!"

"It's called A REMINDER," said Lucy. "Just in case you forgot how good you are."

I glanced at Fernanda, hoping she'd back me up. But she was already on her feet, slipping on her flip-flops and looping her pool bag over her shoulders, as if she didn't have time for our silly arguing.

"Los, I'm gonna check on Mom." She disappeared into their house. "I'm roasting out here." Their screen door slammed behind her.

"I want a bubble tea," said Carlos, rolling the blue chalk between his thumb and forefinger.

"Yeah," I agreed, wiping sweat from the back of my

neck. I could almost taste the ice-cold sweet milky-tea drink and hear the sound of sucking tapioca balls up the wide straw.

"Bubble tea is life," Lucy added, and I felt tears sting my eyes that something so silly as sharing a love for bubble tea made me feel connected to her. "So." Lucy turned to Sully. "The case?"

Sully shuffled his feet. "We've never done cases about friends before."

"Hamlet was a friend," countered Lucy. "We had a case for her."

Carlos looked up. "Not a friend. He's a pig."

"She," Lucy and I corrected at the same time.

"Just think about it, Josie," Lucy said. "Okay? Please?"

I *had* been thinking about it. I was pretty sure I'd made the right decision by not returning to gymnastics this year. I loved the sport, sure. I liked Coach and my teammates. But something felt easier and more carefree this year, with me just focusing on school and helping out at the veterinary clinic, and hanging out with my friends and family. There was less pressure than when I was always worrying about whether I'd nail some new skill.

Besides. Soon gymnastics competitions would start filling up Lucy's weekend schedule, and I didn't want them to fill up mine, too.

I was trying to figure out how to tell Lucy everything I felt inside, for her to understand. I didn't want to hurt her feelings. We'd been best friends for ages, and I wanted to keep it that way.

But still, deep down inside, I didn't think I'd ever go back to gymnastics again, and I was afraid that one day that might break apart our friendship.

"Luce, we'll talk about it later, okay? Mrs. Taglioni is going to be here any minute."

"Yeah, yeah. . . ."

There was a sharpness in Lucy's voice that hadn't been there before. She pulled earphones out of her pocket, unraveling the cords, and popped the buds into her ears.

I scuffed my shoes on the sidewalk, thinking. When we were alone at the farm today, I needed to be honest and tell Lucy how much being at Eastside meant to me, no matter what she said about gymnastics. I needed her to be okay with my decision. We were best friends, and I didn't want that to change, no matter what sports and music and activities we were into. I loved gymnastics, but I loved animals more. It was as simple as that, and as hard as that.

I watched Lucy sit down on the sidewalk, pulling out her earbuds to laugh at some joke Carlos made, and I felt my chin start to tremble. She'd been my best friend for years. But what if my decision to end gymnastics was ending our friendship, too?

Chapter 5

FARM DAY

Taking the train out to the country always felt like a big adventure. Mom sent us off with bagged lunches of PB&J sandwiches, carrot sticks, potato chips, and juice. Mrs. Taglioni, Lucy, and I picked the train car with booth seating so we could eat on the table and watch the scenery change from city to country through the oversized windows. It was hard to believe how much my relationship with my elderly neighbor had changed this year. For most of my life I wouldn't even hang out with Mrs. Taglioni on her front stoop, let alone take a train ride somewhere with her! Thinking about how different things were now, ever since that mischievous little piglet Hamlet came into our lives, brought a smile to my face.

Mike Upton, Mrs. Taglioni's brother, picked us up

from the train station in his oversized, black pickup truck, pulling right up to the front by the platform. He left the truck running while he climbed out to open the passenger door for his sister.

"Happy July, Molly! Hiya, kids!"

"Oh, Mike, your knees," said my neighbor, twisting up her face in one of her signature scowls. I didn't see her looks of disapproval that often anymore.

I glanced at Mr. Upton. He was wearing jeans, so I couldn't see his knees, but now that Mrs. Taglioni mentioned it, it did seem like he was limping a little as he rounded the truck to greet us.

"Just rusty joints, nothing to worry about," he said. "They're always like this after a ride in the old truck."

Mrs. Taglioni made a *humpf* sound under her breath as if she wasn't buying his excuse. I smiled at her brother, trying to melt away the tension in the air. I didn't want anyone starting the day mad at each other, even if their intentions were good. I loved our Saturday adventures together on the farm.

"Good to see you, Mr. Upton!" I said, and Lucy followed suit, adding brightly, "Hi!"

Lucy and I climbed into the back seat, and Mrs. Taglioni sat up front. I loved riding in Mr. Upton's truck.

He rolled down the windows, and the warm, July wind gushed through, swirling around us like a summer hurricane. Since his truck was so tall—or *lifted*, he told us once—we had a great view over the fence lines into acres and acres of farmland outside the city perimeter. This time of year, the whole world seemed vibrant. The air had a sweet, sticky quality to it. Horses and cows grazed in pastures, and the wheat was golden and tall—as you drove by, it looked like the entire field was one giant wave, rolling and swaying.

Lucy bounced her knees and started in on the usual questions right away. "Is Hammie still flipping her bowl? What about that rascally chipmunk? Was he the culprit of Hamlet's missing corncob?"

Sometimes a month felt like a whole year, there were that many updates on the farm. Plus, now with school out for summer, Lucy and I both hoped we'd get to visit the farm more often than once a month. Maybe we'd even learn how to ride horses!

Mr. Upton steered us down a long, winding road and replied, "Oh, Chip? You'll see Chip for sure. . . . He's always foraging for something." Mr. Upton winked at us in the rearview mirror.

"Aw, you named the chipmunk Chip!" said Lucy, and

I felt my face light up with a grin.

"That's a perfect name," I added. I liked that he named all his farm animals—even the wild ones.

"Sure did. He's always hanging around Hamlet's pen. I think that pig of yours doesn't mind a bit, though, even when Chip steals grain from the trough."

I felt my cheeks warm with happiness. I didn't admit it to him, but I also liked that Mr. Upton still called Hamlet *my* pig, even though she'd been living with Mr. Upton seven whole months in the country, and she'd only lived with me for six weeks in the city. But so much had happened when she was a piglet—between bottle-feeding her and bathing her and watching her grow and finding her a forever home—that Hamlet and I just had a special bond you couldn't break, no matter where we both lived. We were connected, through and through.

"Carlos should totally paint Chip a sign, too!" Lucy said, snapping her fingers. "It sounds like they're roomies, ya know?"

I laughed, imagining Hamlet secretly playing with a little chipmunk friend.

Back in the day, when she still lived with me, Hamlet loved napping in front of the fireplace curled up beside Sugar. I felt a sudden, surprising jolt in my chest, wondering for the first time if Hamlet ever missed Sugar, and vice versa. I'd never given much thought to their friendship until now. I filed the thought away. I'd remember to ask Mom and Dad about it tonight when I broke the news about the litter of puppies. Maybe they could drive us out to the farm next time instead of me taking the train, and we'd bring Sugar along so they could play. Maybe even a puppy or two if Dr. Stern gave the okay. Sugar wasn't much of a runner in her old age, but she sure did enjoy sniffing around, and I bet there'd be all sorts of exciting new scents at Mr. Upton's farm.

"This is the best day ever," Lucy whispered, making me laugh.

"You always say that when we come here!"

"Did you have a nice Fourth of July, girls?" asked Mr. Upton.

"Yes!" I nodded. "We had two friends on the parade float this year. And there were fireworks that exploded into stars and hearts. It was so cool."

"Stars and hearts, huh?" Mr. Upton said thoughtfully as he slowly pressed the truck brake at a changing stoplight. "Fireworks sound more advanced these days. We don't get those kinds of fancy shows out here in the country. We did have a little parade down Main Street though. The local high school marching band did a nice performance."

"*Sully* is in marching band," said Lucy with a teasing smile, jabbing my side with her elbow. I bit back a smile and elbowed her back.

"Sully?" said Mr. Upton, glancing at the rearview mirror. "Friend of yours?"

I nodded. "He helped us save Hamlet."

"He's a young writer," added Mrs. Taglioni.

"A writer?" Lucy countered, sounding just as confused as I felt.

"He's always jotting things down in that notebook of his." The old woman patted her short, dark hair, right by where the pigeon-feather hairpin was clipped, making me smile. The hairpin had been an upcycled gift for Handmade Christmas last year, and I used a tuxedo pigeon feather that I'd saved since I was a little kid. It had magic in it. At least, I liked to believe it did.

"Oh—he's not writing stories," Lucy said. "He likes to solve mysteries, stuff like that. He wants to be a detective." She threw me another teasing look. "*And* Josie's boyfriend."

"Lucy!" My cheeks flamed with heat. "No, he doesn't! We're just friends."

"Boyfriend, huh?" Mr. Upton shook his head. "You girls are much too young for boyfriends!"

"Oh, he's super nice, Mr. Upton," I said, trying to overcome my embarrassment. "We've been friends since, like, forever. And he doesn't want to be my boy-friend." I felt my cheeks burn and muttered under my breath, "Not anymore, at least."

"Well, as long as he's a nice boy. Oh dear . . . I'm hav-ing flashbacks to when Margie and Annie were teens!"

I'd never met Mr. Upton's kids—they were grown up and had children of their own now—but I laughed just the same.

"*Tsk-tsk.*" Mrs. Taglioni patted her hair again. "They grow up so fast."

It was about a twenty-minute drive from the train station to Mr. Upton's farm. Most of the time, just like today, Mrs. Taglioni and her brother fell into a private conversation over things Lucy and I didn't know much about. But that was fine by me.

I loved it when I got lost in my thoughts, just listening to the rumbling of the engine and feeling the bounce of the road. I stared out the window, watching the coun-tryside whizz past as we drove to the now-familiar farm in the country where Mr. Upton lived with his various animals. I could still remember how my nerves felt positively electric the first time I drove out here with my family, and how it felt to stroke Hamlet's pink head in the back seat, and the way her ears twitched as she listened to my assurances that she'd love her new home and owner. I had known it deep inside, even before I met Mike Upton and saw the farm, and I wanted her to know it, too.

Things couldn't have turned out more perfectly. Mr. Upton grew to love Hamlet. Even though he never talked about his animals quite like that, I could tell by the tenderness in his voice and how he cared for them.

Right as we turned onto the farm road, I felt Lucy's breath in my ear as she whispered, "I knowwwww you don't want to talk about it, but are you sure you don't want to try out for Level 6? You used to love gymnastics. Don't you remember?" I could tell from her voice that she was starting to get upset, so I turned to face her. Her deep brown eyes were glassy, and she whispered, "I hardly get to see you anymore. I just know that if you came back and practiced some of the skills, you'd level up with us. It's like riding a bike. Muscle memory, you know? Don't you miss all of Coach's weird sayings?!" She kept blinking her eyes, and I knew she was holding back tears. She lowered her voice until it was barely audible. "Gymnastics just isn't the same without you. If you don't come back to the team now, it'll be too late. We'll always be at different stages."

I sighed. "I still love it, Luce. Just because I'm not on the team anymore doesn't mean I don't love the sport. I told you that, remember?"

"Maybe if we watch Simone, Gabi, and Aly videos again, you'll rethink things," she suggested. "I think . . . I mean, you've been away for a while; maybe you forgot what it's like at practice and competition? You know how during summer break, school seems so long ago you don't even remember the tests you were stressed out about? Like that."

"I . . . I don't think it's quite like that, Lucy," I said. "This isn't a vacation for me. It feels more like . . . when you finish a book you loved, and then you pick up a new one that you love, too, but in a different way, if that makes sense?"

"But I miss you! The team misses you."

"I'm right here," I said, squeezing her hand. "You don't need to miss me."

"Yeah. I guess." She sighed. "But . . . if you don't change your mind soon, it'll be too late."

I understood what she meant. Lucy was moving up another level in gymnastics this summer. If I decided to join the gymnastics team again, I'd have to try out to advance another level. If I did that soon, there was still a chance I could move up to Level 6 with Lucy. If I didn't do it now, and came back to the sport in a year or two instead, most likely Lucy and I wouldn't be on the same team ever again.

And we'd been on the same team for . . . forever.

"Don't worry about that now," I said, the words catching in my throat. I took a deep breath. "Let's just have fun today, okay? It's Farm Day! The best day ever, remember?" Lucy nodded. And then I instantly recognized the tall line of oak trees behind her through the window. "Ahhh, we're here!"

"Yay! We're coming, Hammie! You too, Chip!"

As soon as Mr. Upton parked the truck, Lucy and I hopped out and bolted toward the big red barn on Mr. Upton's massive property.

"There are carrots on the shelf for Pogo!" he yelled, referring to his new donkey. "You can give some to Hamlet!"

"Okay, thanks!" I shouted over my shoulder.

"Have fun, girls!" Mrs. Taglioni added. "Don't forget

about a nice snack in an hour!"

"We won't!" shouted Lucy, cupping her hands around her mouth.

The sweet aroma of hay and manure reached my nose first as we zipped past the horses grazing in the fenced-in pastures. "Hi, Andromeda! Hi, Rebel!" I said, giving them a wave. "Hiya, Pogo!" I stopped in my tracks along the tack shelf and wall fans, where there was a bunch of carrots loose in a tin pail. "I promise not to give them all to Hamlet," I assured the donkey, handing two carrots to Lucy as we bolted through the barn.

I always looked for the wooden Hamlet sign first, the one that Carlos had painted. It's the perfect shade of rose pink and written in careful, cursive swirls.

"Hamlet!" I squealed, dropping to my knees at the wooden gate. My pig, once so small I could cradle her in my arms like a baby, was now an adorably huge porker, probably two or three hundred pounds. Maybe even more!

Hamlet popped her snout through the gate opening and oinked loudly by way of greeting. I loved the feeling that she recognized me every time. She nuzzled against my arm, and I stroked her back. Despite her size, Hamlet still looked a lot like the little piglet I had cared for:

mostly pink, with some gray spots along her back, and fine white hairs all over her body.

"She's really shedding now," I said, raising my hand and showing Lucy the strands of loose white hair stuck to my palm.

"Hi, Hammie!" Lucy said, scratching behind the pig's ear. Hamlet squealed happily in response. "You sure that's normal?" she asked, giving Hamlet's patchy hair a once-over.

"Yep. Mr. Upton said so. Pigs shed, especially in the summer."

"Hammie, where's your little friend Chip?" Lucy squinted her eyes and searched the pen. "Here, Josie, let's swing open her gate."

We unhinged the pigpen gate like we normally did. Hamlet could be a real slowpoke when she felt like it, especially in the heat, but I knew how smart and fast she was. Hamlet had a strong sense of smell, and if there was one thing that could make her bolt, it was the smell of lunch. Especially corn—her favorite! Hamlet always loved Mrs. Taglioni's freshly baked corn bread. One time when the scent wafted across our little backyard in the city, Hamlet jumped the fence and destroyed all the plants, just trying to get a taste. Now she was too

big for that kind of mischief, but if she caught a whiff—
whoosh!—she'd burst into a heavy, rolling gallop.

"All right, Hammie, here you go," I said. "How's your food looking?" Her trough was empty, but she'd likely already scarfed down her breakfast because Mr. Upton did the rounds twice a day. Plus, Hamlet wasn't the type of pig to save anything for later. She was a gobbler! Mr. Upton had a watering system rigged to the barn, so it automatically pumped a constant flow of fresh water from the nearby well into the animals' water buckets in the barn and pasture enclosures.

"Drink lots of water, Hammie—it's hot out today. Ah, that breeze feels good." Lucy tugged the neck of her shirt and fanned herself. "It's sooooo brutal out."

"Yeah," I agreed. "Mrs. Taglioni said she's making lemonade for us. . . . She said it's gonna be over ninety today." I patted Hamlet firmly on the back and scratched right on her gray spots, making her rump wiggle. Lucy and I laughed. Hamlet's tail swished back and forth, swatting away buzzing flies, and her ears twitched as she listened to us. "Want to take Hamlet for a walk?"

Hamlet was a real farm pig now, but we still liked to put a harness around her body and walk her around the property. Mr. Upton said that was fine with him as long as we kept a close eye on her. I knew Hamlet could be naughty, but I liked to think she was so happy having me nearby that she'd always choose to stay at my side.

"Yeah!" said Lucy. "Let's take her over there, and sit in the shade under the oak tree? I'll grab her leash and harness!" Lucy pulled them off a nearby nail in the wall. We clipped them on and walked Hamlet up the hill. "Do you think Mr. Upton would care if we gave her a bath?"

"No way. He knows how much Hamlet loves the water on a hot day. Let's fill up her baby pool!"

"Good idea."

We spent the rest of the afternoon hosing down Hamlet, letting her play in the wet, muddy grass underneath the shady oak trees, and laughing at her delighted oinks, snorts, grunts, and squeals. Every time we tried to wash off her dirt-caked body, she rolled back on the ground. We finally gave up in a fit of giggles.

Suddenly I had an idea. "Wait here with Hamlet!" I bolted down to the barn, where Mr. Upton had once shown me the bin of sports equipment in the tack room. Inside, I found an old orange Frisbee, and I raced back to the grassy area with it tucked under my arm.

"Oh no," said Lucy, her lips curling into a sideways

grin. "You can't let her off the leash! What if she runs off?"

I gave Hamlet a once-over. She lifted her nose in the air, as if investigating the Frisbee. I let her sniff it, and her body wiggled and she swished her tail. "Nah. I think she'll be fine. Amelia and Lou taught her this trick, remember?"

Lucy didn't look convinced. "She's pretty fast for a big old hog."

I laughed and gave Hamlet a big pat on the back. "Behave, all right, Hammie? Now let's see if you've still got it!" I waved the Frisbee to catch her attention. Hamlet's mouth hung open a little in a way that almost looked like she was smiling, exposed teeth and all.

"Think she'll catch it?" asked Lucy, grinning.

I pulled an extra carrot from my pocket. "Hamlet will do anything for food!" I snapped the carrot in half. "Unclip her leash? Because there's only one way to be sure. Let's go, Hamlet!"

Lucy set the pig loose. Hamlet trotted my way, her snout rooting for the carrot in my hand. I gave her one piece, and after she chomped it up real good, I ran several feet down the pasture with the Frisbee to my chest. "Ready, set, GO, HAMLET, GO!"

I spun out the Frisbee. It soared high in the sky. Hamlet picked up the pace to a hog gallop and leaped right as the Frisbee torpedoed toward the grass, catching it in her teeth.

Lucy and I couldn't stop laughing. "Good ol' Hamlet!" I said as she circled back to me. I gave her a pat on the rump. "Such a smart piggy!" Hamlet burrowed her nose into my pocket, snatching out the other half of carrot I had tucked inside. "Hammie!" I scolded, clipping her leash back on the harness. "Bad manners! You're supposed to wait until I give you the treat."

We walked around the farm for a bit, but the sun soon tired us out. Hamlet stretched out in a patch of shade, and I lay down on the grass beside her, twisting her long leash in my fingers. "Wouldn't it be cool to live on a farm?" I said to Lucy, sighing.

Lucy plopped down next to me, following my gaze into the trees above. "Maybe, I guess. But wouldn't it be boring, you know, after a while? There's not much to see or do here, besides hanging out with Hamlet and Pogo and the horses. I mean, I'd probably get bored. Eventually."

I tucked my hands behind my head and stared up into the oak tree. The leaves overhead rustled in the hot

July breeze, and I closed my eyes, listening to all the sounds of the farm. I could never get bored here. I could hear the faint whirr of the barn fans, in the distance, and the high-pitched notes of the wind chimes on the front porch of the house, and Hamlet's oinks and snores right beside me. It couldn't have been more different from the sounds of the city, with the constant whoosh of cars, honking horns, sirens, and street noise. And in my house? The Shilling family was practically world-famous for noise, with my brother home for the summer, and my sisters always squabbling about something.

"You're being quiet," Lucy said, propping up on her side.

"Oh, just thinking."

"Josie Shilling!" She burst out laughing. "You're *always* thinking. You live inside your head!"

I blew a stray hair from my eyes. "I was wondering how the puppies are doing today." Lucy pulled out her phone and tapped a phone number on her Received Calls list. "What're you doing?" I asked.

"Helping you. Here."

I pressed the phone against my ear, listening to it ring. "Hello! Thank you for calling Eastside Veterinary Clinic!" said a cheerful voice. I could hear the puppies faintly in the background, with their high-pitched *yip*s and *rawf*s! I grinned.

"Miss Janice? Hi, it's Josie. I'm just checking in on the puppies."

"Oh, honey, they're doing just fine," Miss Janice gushed. "Aren't they the sweetest little things? Sure make quite the mess and racket, but Dr. Stern checked them all out, and they're in great health. Are you coming by to pick them up today?"

"No," I said. "Tomorrow." I met Lucy's eyes. Even though she couldn't hear Miss Janice on the other end, I knew she was sensing my anxiety. It was part of what made her such a good friend.

"Wonderful, hon. Okay then. Well, they'll be happy to see you, that's for sure. I let them out for a bit of exercise, but some parakeets came by to say hello, and one of the puppies climbed up on a chair and stuck its paw in the aquarium—"

I laughed. "It was probably Rocky. He likes to climb."

"And then this other pup, do you hear her going on and on in the background? All that yelping? It's like she constantly wants to share her opinion. And she's had two accidents already. She doesn't seem to like the puppy pads."

"That sounds like Babbles," I said. "Thanks for keeping an eye on them, Miss Janice. Sorry it's a lot of extra work for you today!"

"It's all right, hon. I leave soon. And they're darling."

"Have a great evening, Miss Janice! And thank you again!"

I tapped End on the call and handed the phone back to Lucy. Having a cell phone sure made some things easier!

"Thanks," I said.

"Feel better?"

I patted Hamlet's belly. "Definitely. The puppies are doing great. But I still need to figure out a way to tell my parents about them . . . and get their permission to foster them for two weeks."

"Hmmm. We need thinking music. I'll make a play-list."

I laughed. "Well, if I'm always thinking, *you're* always making a playlist."

"Wait until you hear this mash-up I made. I totally think Coach should make a routine to this. . . ." She trailed off, maybe because she didn't want to fight about gymnastics anymore.

I looked up into the clouds and didn't push the conversation. Sometimes I helped Lucy practice her songs and take a video of herself lip-syncing, but she didn't often talk to me about the app because she knew I didn't have a phone to do it with her. It felt like her interest in music was one more thing pulling our friendship apart.

"Girls! Time for lemonade and watermelon!" Mrs. Taglioni called through the open window of the farmhouse kitchen. "And Mike says to put Hamlet back before you come in, please!"

As if Hamlet could understand Mrs. Taglioni's words, the pig slowly rolled onto her hooves. I laughed. She knew we'd give her more carrots when we secured her back in her pen. Hamlet sure was living the life out here.

I was, too.

Even though I was having fun with Lucy, an unsettled feeling bubbled in my stomach. I knew I couldn't stay on Mr. Upton's farm forever, and that things would be different as soon as we got back home.

Chapter 6

PUPPY LOVE

The next morning, I sat outside on the patio with a book, trying to muster up the courage to ask my parents about fostering the litter of puppies. It was just after church, and I could almost feel the clock ticking toward evening, when I'd promised to pick up the puppies from Eastside.

Mom was sitting next to me when her cell phone rang. "Hi, Cassandra," she said. "How're you?"

I snapped my book closed. Uh-oh.

"We missed seeing Lou this past week," Mom continued. "Yes, Millie's been loving soccer. Oh, just three hours, but it's every day, so that's nice. Gets her energy out. You know Millie. She wants to be a goalie!" I nervously bit my nails. "Oh, I see. So he'll be at his grandmother's this weekend? Well, he's welcome here anytime this summer. Millie has really missed him."

Okay, I'd had enough of this Amelia and Lou talk. My nerves couldn't take it anymore. I made a grabby hands motion to my mom. I needed that phone, and I needed it right now, before Dr. Stern blabbed about the puppy news to my parents!

Mom raised her finger and mouthed, *Hold on*.

I rapped my fingers on the table. Okay. If Dr. Stern brought up the puppies, I could just pretend they were regular puppy patients, couldn't I? Mom wouldn't really know the difference between "my puppies" and "clinic puppies."

Even though there was A. Very. Big. Difference.

"Yes, here you go. She's right here." Mom handed me the phone, whispering, *"Patience, Josie! Good grief!"* and returned to drinking her cup of coffee. I pressed my ear against Mom's phone and said, "Hi, Dr. Stern!"

"Josie, I'm glad I caught you this morning." Her even-tempered voice helped calm my nerves, especially with my parents sitting next to me and the big secret hanging between us. Thank goodness Lou wasn't around this week, or he would have told Amelia, and she'd definitely have spilled the beans by now! "I just want to follow up on the puppies."

"Okay, great!" I said, trying to respond with very general words. I couldn't go inside, because all my siblings were around and they were even *nosier* than my parents! "How's, uh, everything, you know, going?"

"Very well. All the patients have been released to their owners, so it's just the puppies here now."

I glanced at Mom. Her eyes were closed, but if I knew my mom, her ears were wide open. "Okay, awesome!"

"Have you spoken with your parents about them yet?"

My shoulders sagged. "Um, no. Not yet."

"Josie, remember our deal." Dr. Stern's voice was firm but kind. "You need your parents' permission to care for the puppies, and they have to be out of the clinic by tonight. I'm trusting that you'll talk with them as soon as possible, because if they don't approve, we need to figure out an alternate plan ASAP."

I watched Dad flip another page of the newspaper.

"I will, Dr. Stern."

"Will you please have your mother text or call me after you've talked about the puppies? It's a big responsibility, so I want to ensure she knows what dog fostering will require of you."

I exhaled. "No problem."

"Have a good morning, Josie! And with any luck, I'll see you in a few hours."

I frowned. I needed all the luck I could get. I hung up and handed the phone back to Mom.

"You seem . . . jumpy," Mom said. "Everything okay at the clinic?"

"Me? Jumpy?" I straightened my shoulders, as if I was in a gymnastics competition, walking tall and confident. "Nope, all good."

Breathe. Breathe. Breathe.

"What did Dr. Stern want?"

I curled my toes in my flip-flops, letting them dangle off my feet. "Just to go over the patients at the clinic. She leaves for a conference tomorrow, so I told her I'd come by today and . . . check on the animals."

I cracked my knuckles. This was my chance. *Tell them about the puppies, Josie! Tell them!*

But I couldn't.

Mom frowned as she stirred a sweetener packet into her coffee mug. "Josie, I know you're a wonderful help to her, but remember you're only twelve. Dr. Stern has paid employees to do that sort of thing. Don't let this extracurricular activity of yours turn into a full-time job, okay?"

I swatted away a fly that was buzzing around our table. "Don't worry, Mom. I won't."

"And doesn't Dr. Stern have an assistant this summer? What's his name?" asked Dad.

I matched Mom's scowl. "Daniel. He's the veterinary technician."

Mom tapped her password to unlock her cell and paused over the telephone icon. "I was thinking you could come with me to the community center later today, Josie. They're doing a beginners' pottery class."

"Um, what? I don't even like pottery."

Mom shrugged. "Have you tried it? Could be fun. Maybe I should call Cassandra back, just to let her know we have some family plans today. . . ."

I felt myself start to panic. I realized I was pacing the concrete patio like Storm the cat in her cage. Lucy had music and gymnastics. Carlos had art. Fernanda had coding and swimming. Sully had basketball and his detective work. Animals were *my* special thing, and I liked it that way. I exhaled and tried to speak calmly.

"Mom. Dad. I really want to check on the animals,

okay? I love doing it. And it's no big deal. I'm good at it!"

"I know you are, Josie." Mom thought for a minute. "I'd like to come by the clinic with you today then, so you're not alone." She smiled. "I like animals, too, you know. And I care about how you spend your time."

Well . . . maybe she just needed to *see* the puppies. Hear their yelps and touch the soft brown-and-black fur on their bodies. Mom wouldn't be able to say no after she held one and felt it lick her cheek and snuggle against her chest.

"That's a good idea," said Dad.

"You know, that's actually a great idea," I decided, a big grin lighting up my face. "You almost done with your coffee?"

By the time we got to Eastside Veterinary Clinic, Miss Janice was wrapping up for the day. Sundays were always shortened days at the clinic. She gave me a wink and said, "Want to show your mom around, introduce her to the animals? Dr. Stern is going over her conference materials."

I took a deep breath.

It was now or never.

The seven puppies were divided between the crates. Almost all the puppies were snoozing up against each other. Babbles yelped, pawing at the metal door. The one I still hadn't thought of the perfect name for—Number Seven—began to whine. I grinned. Maybe she recognized me!

"Oh, aren't these the sweetest little things," cooed Mom. "No wonder you're excited to spend time here!"

My heart soared. We were off to a good start. "Want to hold one?"

The hinges creaked as I snapped open the lock, and the resting puppies sprang to life, making me smile even though my insides felt like popcorn.

"Hi, little guys!" I said. "Wake up! It's time to play!"

I set them down one by one on the tiles and then remembered to ask Miss Janice to lock the front door. "It's okay if I let them roam around, right, Miss Janice?"

"Yes, Miss Josie!"

I smiled even bigger. I liked that she called me that, *Miss Josie*. It made me feel like I was important here, too. "I'll be right back," Miss Janice said. "Watch the lobby for me?"

"Sure!"

Once all the puppies were loose on the floor tiles, they happily explored, sniffing all the new scents and jumping up against Mom's bare legs. She laughed.

"Tell me about them, Josie!" Mom leaned down to pet Tugger. As she rubbed his fur, he licked her knuckles.

"Tugger is . . . well, he's the tugger," I giggled. "He'll chew pretty much anything."

"And this one?"

"Houdini! He's the escape artist."

"Sounds like another animal we know and love," Mom said, winking, and I knew she was thinking about how Hamlet always used to escape her cave.

Right then and there, Mom surprised me by sitting down on the tiled floor and letting the puppies sniff at her blouse and lick her arms and crawl right into her lap. She laughed and rubbed their furry backs and nestled one of them, Speedy, right up against her neck. I smiled so big, my cheeks hurt.

"It's hard to believe Sugar was ever this small," Mom said.

"How old was she when we got her?"

"Hmmm. Maybe eight or nine weeks?"

"Dr. Stern thinks these puppies are around eight weeks old."

"Is that right?" Mom asked. I explained to her how the puppies had arrived at the clinic in a giant box with a letter addressed to me. She hung on my every word and smiled when I was done telling the story.

"You know, I didn't even want a dog back in the day," Mom said. "Your grandmother gave us Sugar."

"She did?" I grinned. "No one ever told me that before. I just assumed you and Dad bought her from a breeder or something."

"Oh no." Mom laughed. "You were only a few months old . . . and with Tom, Ellen, and Sarah being so young, you can imagine how wild it felt in our little townhouse! I couldn't wrap my brain around potty training a *puppy*, too. No way."

"Yeah. I'm sure. So why did Grandma give her to you guys, if you didn't want a dog?"

"Oh, something about a neighbor's dog having a surprise litter—I can't remember all the details now. But before I knew it, your dad was driving back from Chicago with a puppy in the front seat. It seems like a lifetime ago." Mom's words choked up in her throat, and her eyes took on a watery-glass sheen. "It might sound strange, but Sugar helped me raise you all," she continued, her tone softening. "She's always been so tender and sweet with you kids. It's strange now, thinking about it. I didn't want Sugar in the beginning, but she turned out to be exactly what we needed." Mom smiled at me. "Kinda like Hamlet."

"Yeah." I smiled back. Then I sighed. "I promised Dr. Stern I'd find these puppies homes within the next few weeks. She really doesn't have the space here to keep them long-term, plus she's too busy with her patients."

Mom bit her lip. "Is that right . . . ?"

"Those pint-sized puppies need a mama," said Miss Janice in her strong, matter-of-fact voice, reappearing at the clinic desk. "It's a darn shame they're so little, cooped up in these kennels. . . . And with Dr. Stern leaving for her conference, I suppose they'll just have to go to the pound tonight. . . ." When Mom wasn't looking, Miss Janice winked at me. Ha! She was so clever.

Mom studied the puppies for another moment and then got back to her feet. She adjusted her purse strap on her shoulders and said, "You know, Miss Janice? I think you're right."

I shot Mom a confused look. "Right about what?"

"These puppies need a mama. Have any extra collars and leashes around here that we can borrow?"

I grinned so big, it was like I was grinning with my

heart, too. "Sure do. Right, Miss Janice?"

The woman was already one step ahead of us. She smiled and handed me seven thin, red leashes, each with a hand-tied collar loop at the end.

Chapter 7

SEAL THE DEAL

"Absolutely not." Dad stood in the living room, shaking his head slowly at first and then faster. "I don't see why they're your responsibility instead of Eastside's. Can't Cassandra just deal with them?"

Mom smiled brightly. "Nope!"

Dad sighed, and I explained, "The clinic can't keep them, Dad. Whoever found them trusted me to take care of them. I just need to foster them until they're old enough to go to real homes. Fostering is very . . . temporary. And I'm super responsible. Look—I think Sugar likes the company! Dogs are pack animals, you know."

Dad's face paled as he watched Rocky jump into his recliner in the living room, curling up on the soft leather. Then his gaze shifted to Sugar, who was sleeping on the rug with two other puppies snuggled against her stomach.

His lips pressed together in a thin line. "Have they had shots yet?"

"Have WHAT had SHOTS?" bellowed Amelia, bounding through the front door, kicking off her soccer cleats into the hall closet. *Thwack! Thump!* As she noisily peeled off her socks and shin guards, the noise attracted Speedy's attention. The fast little puppy bounded down the hallway, slipping on her paws and barreling right into Amelia's leg.

"AHHHH! WE GOT A PUPPY?!" Amelia screeched in delight. From my perspective on the floor, I could see her lift Speedy into her arms, cooing into the puppy's ear. "Oh, it's SO cute!! What kind of puppy is it? How old? Boy or a girl? Does it get along with Sugar?"

"It's not really *our* puppy," Mom explained, moving toward the hallway. "Josie is taking care of her while she tries to find a permanent home. We're going to be a foster family for a little while."

Amelia made a face. "What's a foster family?"

"It means we're in charge of her for a short period of

time," I said. "Until they're old enough to get adopted. Dr. Stern says that should be in less than two weeks from now."

I emphasized *less than* and sneaked a glance at Dad's reaction. He was busy pulling Houdini out from underneath the couch. "No, no—these are my new slippers!" He lifted Tugger off his feet and placed him next to Sugar. "Hamlet ruined my last pair, and you are not getting these!"

I didn't bother reminding Dad that she didn't technically ruin them. He *gave* Hamlet his slippers when she went to live at the farm, so that she'd always have a reminder of our family in her pen.

Amelia nestled her nose against the little puppy's, as if she was trying to speak in a language the dog would understand. "You said *her*, right, mom? It's a girl puppy?"

Mom broke into a sideways smile, the sly kind that told me she was either reacting to Amelia's excited energy or Dad's continued scowl. "Yes, Millie, that puppy's *one* of the girls," Mom said. "Josie named her Speedy. Isn't that cute? Because she's really fast, kind of like you, actually. Two Speedys!"

"Aw! Speedy, I like that."

I grinned. I couldn't believe Mom actually remembered

which puppy was which! That had to be a good sign. I'd remember to put it down in the new Case File, once I told the Three Stoops crew about what was going on. I couldn't wait to show them!

"Wait a second!" Amelia squealed. "You said ONE of the girls. . . ." She looked down the long hall and stared at me sitting on the floor of our living room, a pile of furry pups in my lap. "Ahhhhh! More puppies! Are they ALL staying here?!"

"No," said Dad.

"Everything's settled and everything's fine," said Mom, throwing him a look. He sighed and disappeared up the stairs.

"Mom, I don't want Dad to be mad." I felt the ball of excitement inside my chest start to deflate.

"I'll talk with him, Josie. We're only committing to fourteen days, and you know what? I love puppies! So. Just prove to Dad that you can take care of them, just like you took such wonderful care of Hamlet, okay? Then he has nothing to be concerned about! Now, let's see. Where's Sugar's old crate? I know we packed it up some-where. . . ." She placed her hands on her hips, thinking. "Maybe Dad stuck it in the attic with the holiday dec-orations. I'm going to look for it while you and Millie watch the puppies. We can't have them all loose, all the time, okay, girls? And Josie, you'll get the word out that they're up for adoption soon?"

I reached over and gave Mom a big hug. "Thanks, Mom. I will. I have . . . a plan. I think."

"Good. I like your plans." She ruffled my hair. "This is the happiest Sugar's been in a while, don't you agree?" She guided my chin gently toward the dogs. Sugar's tail was lightly thumping against the floor—*bop bop bop*— while the puppies sniffed and snuggled against her.

"Awwww, the puppies probably miss their mama," said Amelia.

"You know, I think you're right," I said, studying them in amazement. "And Sugar is so gentle with them!"

Mom gave me a final squeeze. "You have a good heart, Josie Shilling. Now. Off to find that crate! Girls, keep a *very* close eye on them, okay? It's not puppy proofed in here."

"Yep!"

"Did the others see them yet?" asked Amelia after Mom left. Speedy tugged at her soccer shirt with her teeth, making her squeal. "OW! She's got sharp teeth!"

"Yeah, puppies play-bite. They don't mean any harm by it, but their teeth are sharp for sure. It's part of why we need to keep socializing the puppies with people and other animals, so they learn boundaries and how to be well-behaved dogs. Once they've had all their shots, that is. Right now we should keep them pretty close to home and limit the strangers and dogs they meet. And no, the others haven't seen them yet." I glanced at the front door, where I knew my brother and older sisters would appear pretty soon. Tom's shift was almost over, and Ellen had gone to the library for a quick study session for her online college class. Who knew where Sarah was.

Amelia scolded Speedy as the puppy tried to leap from her lap. "Well, they're *not* going to like them."

I sighed, knowing she was probably right. "Too bad for them. Because the puppies are here for two weeks, no matter what they say."

I wasn't quite sure about that, but it sounded good.

Amelia grinned. "Speedy can sleep in our room! She's my favorite."

"She's only your favorite because you haven't held the others."

"Nuh-uh! It's because she's the fastest, like me."

"Mom says they all have to sleep in the crate, so don't get any ideas like sneaking them into our room or anything."

"You sneaked Hamlet into our room a few times."

I covered up a smile with the back of my hand. She had a point, but I wasn't about to get in trouble and risk losing the chance to foster the litter. "That's different. She was only one pig, Millie."

She rolled her eyes. "Still sneaky, though."

"Who's sneaky?" Sarah's voice carried into the living room, and I looked up just in time to see her chomping down on a chip, eyes wide open. "You've. Got. To. Be. Kidding. Me. MORE ANIMALS, JOSIE?! What, are you doing an animal reality show now, too?"

My face warmed with heat. Even though I didn't think Mom would go back on her word to let us foster the puppies, I couldn't have Sarah on *Dad's* side! If fostering went to a family vote, I'd be doomed. The puppies would be at Eastside—or maybe even the overcrowded city pound—in no time.

"It's just temporary," I said. "Aren't they SO cute? And look, they're keeping Sugar company!" I pointed to our golden retriever. It was becoming my go-to move. Sugar lifted her head. She sniffed at the puppies, licking and cleaning their fur, just like their real mom might've done.

Sarah rolled her eyes. Her icy heart apparently didn't crack at the sight of adorable puppies. She popped another chip into her mouth. "Sure, they're cute, but this place is going to smell like dog pee. It's gross, Josie. Can you stop bringing home stray animals already? Whyyyyy does our family have to be so embarrassing? I'm going to be hearing about this all year, like with Hamlet. You have no idea the stuff kids were saying at school about us when that pig was around." Her phone buzzed, and she fired off a return text message.

"We're not embarrassing! That's so mean, Sarah," said Amelia, hugging Speedy closer. I sighed. It seemed as if doing the right thing, like taking care of innocent homeless puppies, was also making my home life a lot more complicated.

"Sarah, don't be so dramatic. It won't smell like dog pee." Mom appeared in the living room doorway. It was like that sometimes when you lived with a bunch of people in a tiny townhouse. People always popped into rooms and conversations without warning. "Josie will teach them to use pee pads and eliminate outside. Ta-da, I found the old crate!" She lowered six flat metal wire sides to the floor and began to put the crate together. It was an extra-large crate, but after glancing at the seven puppies jumping on top of Amelia, clawing at the wool rug, and sniffing Sugar's belly, I started to doubt that they'd be comfortable inside.

"Mom . . . ," I began as I helped her assemble the crate by the bay window overlooking the city street, "we might need to make a puppy pen."

"What's that?"

"A bigger enclosed space for them, like the cave we made for Hamlet in that nook under the stairs. I mean, the puppies are tiny and snuggly with each other, so I'm sure this huge crate will be fine for now, but I don't know . . . in another week or so they might be a lot bigger. . . ."

I swear Mom's eyes twinkled. "Let's just figure it out day by day, okay? Maybe a few of them will adopt quickly. We'll give this crate a shot and then reassess."

Reassess. I liked that word, and the idea that trying something else was always an option. While I held two metal sides together, Mom slid a long rod through their adjacent holes, securing them.

"If they grow so fast, the puppies can just go out back," Dad called out from upstairs. "In the doghouse!"

"NOOOO!" Amelia and I exclaimed at the same time.

"The wood is smelly and rotting away!"

"And there are huge spiders!" Amelia added, eyes widening. "The daddy longlegs kind. It's CREEPY. Not even Sugar likes it in there, and it's *her* house!"

"And the puppies need vaccinations," I added.

"Uh, and there's, you know, predators?" said Sarah, stating it like it was obvious. "A few nights ago, Trish saw a raccoon in the dumpster out back."

"Hey, ho!" boomed a voice from the front door.

"We're home," added another, calmer voice.

Great. Tom and Ellen were here.

"Guess what!" screamed Amelia, zooming into the hallway. "We got puppies!"

"Really?" Tom said, walking into the living room and giving the chaotic scene a once-over. "That's kinda cool. And I'm gonna bet this week's paycheck that our resident Dr. Doolittle took them in!"

Amelia started cracking up, but I'd bet a *million* dollars she had never heard of Dr. Doolittle before. I rolled my eyes. Tom and Amelia had a ten-year age difference between them, but about the same maturity level. "Very funny, Tom," I said.

"They're so cute," said Ellen. "But what're they doing here?"

Amelia babbled off the update and added, "Dad wants to stick them in the scary, icky, spidery doghouse out BACK! And Sarah says there's a raccoon that will get them!"

"Raccoons don't eat dogs." Dad massaged little circles on his temples. "At least, I don't think they do."

"You're right. They don't," said Sarah. "They eat garbage. Like I said."

"Well, if it's a rabid raccoon, it might bite the puppies," considered Ellen. "Raccoons can be aggressive if they're cornered, too. They've got claws and teeth and probably carry countless strains of unfavorable bacteria."

"Unfavorable bacteria?" Sarah rolled her eyes. "Who talks like that?"

"Oh, sorry. *Nasty germs.* Is that easier for you to understand?"

I threw Mom a knowing look. "THAT is how Daniel talks. See what I mean?!"

"Who's Daniel?" asked Dad.

"The annoying vet tech at Eastside."

"Are you calling me annoying?" snapped Ellen.

"Girls, girls!" Mom's stop-sign hand appeared in the air. "Please be kind."

"Anyways, you're all missing the main predator here," broke in Tom. "Let's talk about that owl that lives in the park, by the library."

Dad looked even more confused. "What owl?"

Tom puffed up his lips and exhaled dramatically. "The annoying hooter, Dad. The annoying hooter."

Sarah went back to texting but fired off another snarky comment. "Speaking of annoying, you keep saying things twice."

"It's for emphasis," countered Tom, a wide grin on his face. "My Public Speaking professor said repetition can really drive a point home for the listener. See? It's obviously working."

Sarah looked up, but only for a brief moment. "Aaand you got a D in Public Speaking right?"

"A C plus, Sarah. *C plus.*"

Tom tsk-tsked, as if he was disappointed in her for forgetting his exact grade. I couldn't help but laugh. Even though Tom's constant jokes got old sometimes, they also helped break up the ongoing arguments between my sisters. It was good to have him home this summer.

"Tom has a point," said Ellen, hugging her book to her chest. "An overly repeated point, but he has a point."

"Thank you, O Favorite Sister." Tom cracked his

knuckles as Ellen threw him another scowl. "Wait. What was my point again?"

"About the owl being a danger to the puppies," Ellen said.

"An owl is NOT getting these puppies!" Amelia burst in, her high-pitched voice shaking as if she might cry at any moment. "And I thought *I* was your favorite sister."

"I have three favorite sisters," said Tom.

Sarah looked up, narrowing her eyes. "You have four sisters."

Tom pointed his finger, drawing imaginary squiggly lines in the air. "You ladies are gonna have to guess who didn't make the cut!"

"Um, yeah. Not wasting my brain cells on that one."

"Honey, don't worry," said Mom, tucking a loose strand of hair behind Amelia's ear. "The puppies are much too little and vulnerable to be in the backyard alone. Don't concern yourself with that, okay? Besides, Stephen, don't you remember how we crate trained Sugar? It worked so well back then. . . ."

Amelia eyed the metal crate assembled beside the window. "How does it train them?"

"Dogs don't want to soil where they sleep," explained Mom. "So it helps with housebreaking. And it can help a dog feel safe, too. Crates can reduce separation anxiety, especially for puppies."

"Really?" I raised my eyebrows. "I didn't know that."

"Well, not all puppies, I'm sure, but it's worth a try." Mom smiled brightly.

I hadn't mentioned that I was worried about successfully housebreaking seven puppies, so if a crate would help with that, I was on board. I mentally made a note to myself to visit the library and check out some books on dog training.

"But that's not fair to the puppies," Amelia said. "Who wants to be stuck inside an old crate when you can be sniffing and wrestling and running around?"

"Oh! They won't be in there the whole time, of course. Just when we leave the house, so they're not loose. . . . And probably during mealtime. We don't want seven furry beggars, like Sugar. Now." Mom clapped her hands together. "Josie, what kind of supplies do you need from the pet store?"

"I wanna go to the pet store, too!" Amelia jumped to her feet. "Mom, Dad, can I go with Josie? Please? I won't be trouble, I promise."

"No way." I got to my feet, too, standing tall next to my little sister. "It's like a ten-minute walk and you'll whine the whole time. I'm asking Lucy to come with me."

I stuck my tongue out at her as I gathered up all the puppies and put them in the big crate in the corner. They snuggled in just fine now, at eight weeks old, but I bet they'd be too big soon. I needed to win Dad over so I could make the puppy pen under the stairs as soon as possible.

"Josie!" Mom scolded. "Be kind. Amelia misses her best friend. You should be able to understand how that might feel. . . ." I made a face. I hadn't told Mom about my troubles with Lucy lately, but yeah, I understood how it felt to miss your best friend. Sometimes it felt like I didn't even know mine anymore. "Millie doesn't have a bunch of kids her age on the block like you do," Mom continued. "She's going with you. Now. Josie, are you using your allowance money to get these puppy supplies?"

Ugh! Of course Amelia would not only have to come to the pet store with me, but Mom would want to work out the money details. I had saved up about forty-three dollars in my allowance jar upstairs, under my bunk bed. I wasn't sure exactly how much puppy harnesses and food cost, but I thought I'd be close to covering it.

"I guess. . . ."

"Do the puppies have an adoption fee to cover the cost of their care?" asked Dad, popping into the doorframe. He adjusted his favorite apron around his waist, and the smell of mushrooms sizzling in a pan of olive oil floated into the room.

"I didn't think about that part yet," I admitted.

"Hmmm. Your dad has a good point." Mom nodded. "How about this? I'll lend you fifty dollars now, and after you adopt out a puppy or two, you can pay me back with the funds? I think it's appropriate for you to sell them for a small fee, which would just cover the expenses for caring for them." Her gaze shifted to the large crate in the corner. "If you keep them around much longer, they're going to each need their own dog crate."

"Or a puppy pen," I chimed in.

"Let's not go there," Dad said. "Okay, the spaghetti sauce is calling my name."

"I still want Speedy to sleep in my room." Amelia did a giant lunge, stretching her calves like our living room was a soccer field. "And Josie, I'm still coming with you, so DON'T LEAVE ME!"

Mom gave me a look. "Just the pet store around the corner and toward the bus station, right?" she asked me, and I nodded. "Okay. And here—take my cell phone, too, in case of an emergency. Take Amelia with you and Lucy. Be back for dinner!"

"I'm not a baby, Mom. Lots of my friends do things without their parents. Fernanda and Carlos even take the city bus to the Y sometimes!"

"We know you're not a baby. But still, your dad and I feel better about safety in numbers."

"Fiiiiiine. But I can bring a puppy with us, right? I'll be really careful. I need to know what size collars to get, so it'll be better if we can try one on. Hmm. Maybe I should look at harnesses, too, just in case they slip out of the collars."

I glanced over at Sugar. She used to loved sniffing around the pet store, but nowadays it seemed like too far a walk for her. She snored softly, leaning against my brother's legs.

Houdini and Babbles circled the back part of the crate, sniffing around, until they curled up against each other and closed their eyes. Blue and Rocky whined and pawed at the metal sides, trying to reach for us. "I'll get newspaper and line it in a bit," said Mom thoughtfully.

"Thanks, Mom," I said, reaching for my Velcro wallet on the side table.

"They'll stop whining soon, right?" called out Dad. "And Josie, Amelia, come eat before you go. Food's ready!"

"Okay, Dad!" I yelled back.

After my little sister quickly ate the spaghetti lunch, Mom asked us, "Which puppy are you taking to the store?"

"Hmmm. That one." I pointed toward Seven, the one I hadn't quite figured out yet. Maybe if I spent a little extra time with her, I'd learn more about her personality and come up with the perfect name. I hooked a red leash to Seven's collar and picked her up. "C'mon, pup. Let's go, Amelia."

"Yes, ma'am!" Amelia saluted me, making me laugh. She sure annoyed me half the time, but my sister was also really funny.

Outside, Mrs. Taglioni sat on her front stoop next to her watering can. She dabbed her forehead with a little white cloth and looked up as we hopped down the steps.

"Hello, Josie, Amelia! Still so hot out, isn't it?"

"Yeah," I agreed, just as Amelia pointed to the little fur ball cradled in my arms.

"Look what we got!"

"Oh my heavens!" Mrs. Taglioni placed a hand over her heart. "Where did this puppy come from?"

She said *puppy* like a baby hippopotamus had materialized on her front stoop. I couldn't help but laugh.

We sat down next to our neighbor on the steps. The puppy wiggled into her lap, and Mrs. Taglioni cracked a smile.

"We're flobstering," explained Amelia proudly.

"Flobstering?" asked Mrs. Taglioni, gently stroking the puppy's ears before handing her back to me.

"Fostering," I clarified. "A litter was abandoned over at Eastside Veterinary Clinic. . . . I'm just helping care for them. There are seven puppies in total! I wish we could keep one, but it doesn't seem like my parents are up for that. We have Sugar and all."

I rocked my arms side to side and cradled the furry puppy like a newborn baby. She slowly closed her eyes, nestling against my skin. I loved watching the puppy's little whiskers twitch and nostrils flare, like she was drifting off into puppy dreamland. I wondered what puppies dreamed about. Sometimes Sugar would run or bark in her sleep, like she was chasing an imaginary cat.

"Seven!" Mrs. Taglioni's voice trilled in her signature

shaky voice. "Do they . . . bark?"

Of course she'd be worried about noise, even though these were the cutest puppies I'd ever seen! Eight months ago I would've held back a snarky comment, but today I just laughed. Mrs. Taglioni hated lots of noise, and between the city sounds and having us Shillings as neighbors, she sure dealt with a lot of it.

"They yelp!" said Amelia, and I swear Mrs. Taglioni's eyes widened as big as full moons.

"It's like quiet, adorable yips," I added.

"I see. Well, it is cute. . . ."

The puppy sniffed at her shirt as if the scent of Mrs. Taglioni's lunch still lingered on the fabric. Then Seven raised her nose and caught the aroma of something else in the July breeze and tried to jump out of my arms.

"Oh nooooooo you don't," I said, tightening my hold on her. It was like a flashback of Hamlet's escape last year, when the pig made a terrible mess in Mrs. Talgioni's backyard. I'd had to use all my saved allowance money to pay for the damage. Maybe this puppy wouldn't be strong enough to barrel over planters and a wooden fence like Hamlet, but I knew that you couldn't underestimate an animal's curiosity.

"Mrs. Taglioni, they're only staying with us for two

weeks," I said. "We're trying to find families to adopt them."

I hated to imagine what would happen if I didn't meet the two-week adoption deadline. I'd seen sad movies about animals that end up at the city pound, and what happens to them if they're there too long and the shelters get overcrowded. I didn't know if those terrible stories were true, but I didn't want to find out, either.

Mrs. Taglioni scratched Seven's head, and I grinned. I think the puppy was growing on her!

"These brown markings on the fur above her eyes," Mrs. Taglioni mused. "Just like two lucky copper pennies. What did you name her?"

"She doesn't have a name," I said. "Yet."

"Lucky's a cute name! I always look for lucky pennies on the sidewalk," chimed in Amelia. "The shiniest ones are the luckiest."

"Is that so?" Mrs. Taglioni winked at her.

I smiled and stared down at the puppy for a minute. Holding her in my arms right then did make me feel pretty lucky. "Yeah. I like that. Lucky." I grinned again.

Lucky was the perfect name!

"Where are you off to now, children?"

"I'm helping Josie at the pet store!" said Amelia.

"And hopefully *listening* to me at the pet store."

"Well, doesn't that sound like a fun outing." Mrs. Taglioni brushed her palms across the front of her khaki pants. "I have an appointment in a few minutes, but you enjoy that puppy time. She sure is a sweet little thing." Mrs. Taglioni gave Lucky a gentle pat on the head. "Have a good afternoon, girls."

"Bye, Mrs. Taglioni!"

I set Lucky down on the sidewalk and let her walk next to me. As we went down the block, I heard the slam of a taxi door behind me. When I spun around, a woman dressed up in nice clothes was standing in front of our row of townhouses. I didn't want to be nosy, but Mrs. Taglioni had sure been nosy with my family over the years, so I figured I could linger just one second longer, even though Amelia was tugging on my shirt to move faster.

Whining, already. Typical Millie!

The mysterious woman shook hands with my neighbor and then stood back on the sidewalk in the full sun, taking in our row of old townhouses on the city block. It looked like she was asking Mrs. Taglioni questions as she pointed to things—like maybe the chimney?—and I watched my neighbor's lips move as she answered them, a hand raised across her forehead to block the sun.

I wasn't sure who this fancy lady was, why she was on our block, and why Mrs. Taglioni didn't offer to introduce us, but as we walked the final two blocks to the city pet store, I had a feeling that something was going on next door that we didn't yet know about.

Chapter 8

NEW KID ON THE BLOCK

"What're we buying, anyway?" Amelia said, trying to keep up with my pace.

"You heard me tell Mom already." I rolled my eyes. "You need to be a better listener, Millie. You're always too busy talking."

"I was thinking about that owl hunting the puppies, is all," she said quietly. I felt a tug at my heart. Maybe I was being too hard on her. Amelia was a few years younger than me, after all.

"Okay, fine." I exhaled. "So we need seven harnesses. Food and water bowls. Puppy pee pads, for sure." I ticked off the items on my fingers, trying to make sure I wouldn't forget anything. "Dogs have a natural desire to chew, so we need a few good puppy toys. Otherwise they're going to find things to chew on in the house! And we have to get their identification tags made. . . ."

"Tags like Sugar's? With our phone number on them?"

"Yep. There's this little machine that you stick coins in. Then you type in the information, and it gets engraved in the metal."

Amelia flashed me a grin. "That's cool! I want to do it."

I laughed. "Yeah, it's pretty cool."

Up ahead, I spotted Lucy talking with a girl I didn't recognize. She had long, straight black hair and was wearing a cute outfit of cutoff jean shorts and brand-new white Vans, which made me instantly kick at the sidewalk with my old, worn-in sneakers. I mean, they were downright *embarrassing*, but I'd never thought much about them until now. My big toe was nearly poking through the top on my right shoe!

"Who's that?" asked Amelia, bouncing at my side. I felt a twinge of jealousy. The girl didn't go to Henderson Middle School, the public school I attended with the twins and Sully, so she must be one of Lucy's private school friends. Maybe they were hanging out when I called.

"Dunno," I said.

I watched as Lucy pulled out her cell phone and typed something quickly. Finally, she looked up and gave us a little half wave.

"Hey, Luce! I brought Lucky!"

The other girl turned her head, studying us. Usually I was the tallest girl on the block, but this girl looked about the same height as me. The thing was, she wore her height differently, just like her clothes. Her shoulders were pressed back, and she stood up straight, not all hunched over and self-conscious like me.

"Awww, hi, puppy! Hi, puppy's owner!" The girl bent down and ruffled Lucky's fur.

"We have SEVEN of them!" broke in Amelia. My little sister not only had our brother's speed, she got his chatterbox mouth, too!

"Well, it's a litter," I said, trying to explain, but Lucy interrupted me with a laugh that sounded unusually high-pitched.

"Josie's, like, *really* into animals," Lucy said. I felt my face heat up. It didn't sound like she was giving me a compliment, but she leaned down and let Lucky sniff her hand, so I couldn't be sure.

"Oh. That's cute." The girl looked me straight in the eyes and stuck out her hand, which caught me off guard.

I didn't know any kids our age who actually shook hands. Maybe she was older than Lucy and me.

"I'm Grace Jung."

"Josie Shilling." I shifted my weight to the other leg. Was that . . . *purple eye shadow* she was wearing? I didn't even know how to cover up the pimples that were suddenly appearing on my face, let alone wear eye shadow. I glanced at Lucy, blinking. "Do you two . . . go to the same school?"

"Nope." Grace adjusted the shoulder strap of her pink purse. "I'm new here. We just met. I was exploring the neighborhood while my parents are out doing boring stuff, you know. I left my cell phone charging at home by mistake, so Lucy gave me directions."

"I still can't believe you're an actual singer," gushed Lucy. "That is like my *dream*. I mean, lip-syncing is just me trying it out, you know? I'm working on my performance."

I felt my stomach twist up watching the way Lucy leaned forward, as if she was listening intently to every word out of Grace's mouth. Since when was singing Lucy's dream? I knew she had a bunch of followers on that music app SyncSong, but I'd always thought gymnastics was her dream.

"A singer? Do you have a YouTube channel or something?" I asked. Grace blinked, and I felt myself start to sweat. "Um, I guess that's a no?"

"I mean, I *have* a YouTube channel, but I'm not a YouTube star," Grace said, shrugging. "My dads promised I can record an EP at a studio downtown. They know a producer or something. I'm trying to get a demo tape ready." Her gaze shifted to the stoplight on the next block, as if the bold red light was more interesting than having a conversation with me.

All that music talk was like hearing a foreign language I didn't understand, but I wasn't about to ask more questions and look ridiculous. Instead I just matched Grace's casual tone and said, "Oh, that's cool."

"I can't wait to check out your SyncSongs," said Lucy, tapping on her phone screen. "I just found your account and followed you!"

"Awesome, I'll follow you back when I get my phone." Then Grace glanced at me. "I'll find you on it, too."

"Oh." I felt my cheeks warm again. "I'm not on Sync-Song."

"Josie doesn't even have a cell phone," piped up Amelia.

My little sister was bouncing off to the side, so I knew

she was getting antsy. If we didn't start walking toward the pet store soon, she would find annoying ways to channel that extra energy. Like continuing to babble and embarrass me!

"Five minutes, Millie—just relax."

Grace pointed back and forth at us. "Are you two related?"

"She's my little sister."

"Her *athletic* sister," added Amelia.

I rolled my eyes. "Whatever. Athletic sister."

"How old are you?" Amelia asked her.

"Thirteen," said Grace. "How old are you?"

"Nine."

I unwound Lucky's thin leash from my hand, giving her a little more lead to sniff at the fire hydrant nearby and alongside the iron gate at a neighbor's front stoop. Then I remembered that Grace had said she was new to the neighborhood. I looked up, toward where the shiny new glass high-rise building was located, five or six blocks away. Some old townhouses had been demolished last spring, and this building was built within a few months. I'd heard it was one of those fancy buildings like where Miss Janice lived. "So, Grace, do you live in High Towers Apartments?"

"Josie, you won't believe it!" Lucy broke in. "Grace is moving into *Mrs. Taglioni's townhouse*!"

My head snapped back in surprise. "What're you talking about?"

"At the end of the month, right, Grace?" Lucy said, and the new girl nodded. "It's going to be soooooooo fun having more kids our age on our block. We have to introduce her to the Three Stoops crew. Ooh—maybe now it will be the *Four* Stoops!"

"What's the Three Stoops?" Grace rolled her shoulders back. Lucy started telling her about our friends, where we go to school, and how we meet up on Sully's front stoop a few times a week.

I shook my head, as if trying to shake water out of my ears. "There's got to be a mistake," I said. "Mrs. Taglioni's not moving. I would *know*. I just talked to her."

Lucy shrugged. "Josie, you know we all love your old neighbor, too, but don't worry. I'm sure we'll visit the farm all the time to see Hamlet and see her then, too!"

Huh?

"Who's Hamlet?" Grace looked just as confused as I felt.

"A pig," said Lucy, Amelia, and I at the same time.

"I'll introduce you to my best friend, Lou! Well, when

135

he gets back from camp," added Amelia. "He can throw a baseball really fast."

"That's cool." Grace smiled, as if my little sister was as cute as the puppy. Then she looked at Lucy. "So is that what kids your age do here, sit on steps and hang out? Isn't that—you know—a little *boring*?"

I'm not sure if she meant to sound snobby or not, but Grace was only a year older than us. Maybe only six months older than us. She said "your age" like we were babies!

Lucy shrugged. "Um, I mean, sometimes, yeah." Then her eyebrows rose. "What did you guys do for fun where you're from? We could totally use some new ideas."

What? I crossed my arms over my body. No, we didn't. I liked hanging out on the brick steps just fine. Since when was the Three Stoops too boring for Lucy?

I watched a city bus zoom down the street, feeling myself start to panic inside. Too many changes were happening at once. The puppies, Mrs. Taglioni moving, this new girl Grace. She seemed nice, I guess, and Lucy seemed to like her, but talking to her felt like talking to one of my older siblings, someone more like Sarah, who makes you feel immature and definitely, *definitely* not cool.

"Back in California, we'd go to the mall a lot, or have pool parties at our friends' houses. We lived only twenty minutes from the beach, so everyone would boogie board on the weekends." Grace looked around the neighborhood and made a face. "Guess that's not happening here."

"Ohhhh, boogie boarding! That's so fun. We did that once at Lake Erie," said Lucy.

"The waves are a bit rougher in the Pacific Ocean." Grace laughed, and I felt my cheeks warm, even though she wasn't laughing at me directly. Lucy pressed up on her toes, all wide-eyed and impressed.

"Yeah, there's no beach, mall, or houses with pools here," said Lucy. "Well, there's the community pool at the YMCA, if that counts? Fernanda and Carlos go there a lot. They're on the swim team. So you could always go with them if you get homesick for swimming." Grace sighed, and Lucy quickly added, "So, why'd you guys move to Ohio from California? It sounds *so awesome* there. . . ."

"One of my dads got transferred with his job. We're staying in temporary housing until we can move into the townhouse—" Suddenly Grace screamed at the top of her lungs, making me jump. "Get it off! GET IT OFF!"

I looked down in alarm. Lucky was squatting. A wet, yellow liquid spread across the brand-new white fabric of Grace's Vans, right where the puppy had peed on them.

I quickly tugged back Lucky's leash, but it was too late.

Grace's shoe was soaked in urine!

"I'm *sooooooooo* sorry!" I cried. I looked around frantically for something to blot on her shoes, but I had nothing. Nothing!

Amelia erupted in giggles, wrapping her arms around her waist. "Ewwwww! That is so gross! Wait until I tell Tom about this!"

"Millie!" I scolded, sweat beading across my forehead. "I'm so sorry, Grace. Lucky's a really young puppy. We haven't started housebreaking her yet! I'm really sorry! I'll clean your shoes for you!"

Lucy scrunched up her nose, and I knew how grossed out she must be, too. Grace wouldn't stop staring at her Vans, eyes blazing with fury. She used the top of one shoe to peel the yellowed sneaker off her bare foot.

Please say something, I wanted to beg her. *Anything!*

"We have a hose! In my backyard, right over there!" I couldn't stop rambling to fill the embarrassing, urine-soaked silence. "I'm so sorry! Here, give it to me. I'll go clean it. I'm used to washing blankets and towels with, um, pee, at the veterinary clinic. It'll be spotless, promise! Er—what shoe size are you? You could wear my shoes home while I wash it. Here. Let's trade."

Grace met my gaze with an intense stare. Then she spun around, whipping her long hair over her shoulder, and walked down the sidewalk.

"Uhhhhh . . ." I exchanged a worried look with Lucy.

Lucy called out, "Wait! Grace, where're you going?"

"SHOES CAN BE WASHED, YOU KNOW!" Amelia yelled, cupping her hands around her mouth.

Grace didn't bother looking over her shoulder. We all watched as Grace walked to the corner, kicked off the other shoe, and tossed them both into the garbage can.

Chapter 9

BREAKING NEWS

"Is she seriously walking home barefoot right now?" I asked Lucy, horrified.

"I think so. And there's probably, um, broken glass around? She's not in California anymore." Lucy cupped her hands around her mouth and yelled, "WATCH OUT FOR GLASS!"

Grace didn't turn around. She just kept walking. We watched her until she disappeared around the corner a few blocks away. I knelt down and picked Lucy up into my arms, softly stroking her head. It was no use getting mad at her—puppies were puppies. They had accidents!

Ugh. And this accident just happened to be on my new neighbor's new shoes.

"This is bad," I said. "Real bad."

Lucy swept a hand across her cheek, brushing away a strand of hair. "Definitely bad."

"Those sneakers looked new."

"Totally new."

"What am I going to do?" I stared at Lucy. "Grace hasn't even moved in next door, and she hates me already!"

My best friend frowned. "Yeah, this is a bummer. I really like Grace. We were going to do a SyncSong together! Here, I'll just text her. . . ."

I bit my lip, trying to play it cool and set Lucky down on the ground to sniff. "Oh, you have her number, too?"

Lucy nodded as if it was no big deal, but this little thing felt like another wedge between us.

"Hey!" called out a voice from behind us.

I turned around. "Hey, Sully." Lucy gave me a knowing look, and I felt my cheeks grow hot again. Ugh! She was always overanalyzing me in front of him! It was so embarrassing.

"Cool! You got a puppy?" Sully bounded up and started scratching Lucky's head. "Aw, I've missed having a little pet around. He's no Hamlet, but he's pretty cute."

"She," Lucy and I corrected at the same time.

Lucky tugged on the leash, jumping all over Sully and licking his face. I laughed, which was better than crying—what I had been about to do before Sully walked up. I exhaled and tried to stay calm. Today wasn't going the way I planned at *all*.

"This is Lucky," I told him. "I actually have some news about her. . . . I was going to call a Three Stoops meeting to explain everything."

"Good idea," said Lucy, nodding. She reached for the old pink bike chain on the ground near the front door and looped it around the gate. It was our Three Stoops tradition for making a meeting official. "Let's call it right now. An emergency meeting. We have lots to talk about. I'll text the twins."

"Aw, can I come to the meeting?" asked Amelia. "I never get to do anything fun."

"Lucy, we have to get to the pet store. I don't think we can have a meeting right now—"

"Oh. Right!" Amelia snapped her fingers. "But it's an emergency meeting. Lucy said so."

I sighed. If I chose the pet store over a Three Stoops meeting, I'd probably never hear the end of it—from Lucy or Amelia. "Okay, but only a *quick* one. We really gotta run to the store. But Amelia, you're not coming to the meeting! You can go kick the soccer ball in our back-yard."

"But I'm part of the stoops, too," Amelia protested.

Lucy patted Amelia on the head. "You can stay, Millie."

I scowled. What was with her? First she acts like Grace is the coolest person on the planet, and now she wants my annoying little sister to stay for a confidential Three Stoops meeting? It's like Lucy was doing whatever she could to *not* be alone with me. Realizing that my best friend felt the weight of tension between us, too, and that it wasn't just in my mind, made me feel worse about our friendship.

"No way," I said, my tone sour. "Millie, just go home."

"Aw, come on, Josie," said Lucy. "Her best friend is away. It's fiiiiiine."

I stared at her. "You sound like my mom."

"YAY!" Amelia clapped as if Lucy's permission was the only one she needed.

Beep!

"Grace texted back!" exclaimed Lucy.

I craned my neck to see her phone screen, but she cra-dled it close so I couldn't make out the words. "What'd she say?"

"Who's Grace?" asked Sully.

I looked up. I'd almost forgotten he was standing right there!

Lucy groaned. "Um. *Ohhhhh*."

"What'd. She. Say?!"

Lucy tapped her phone screen off. "She's definitely mad. And they were definitely new shoes."

"It was pretty gross," said Amelia.

"Millie, stop talking and just go grab Grace's shoes from the garbage, okay?" I threw her a look. "I'll toss them in the washer at home."

Amelia put her hands on her hips. "I'm *not* climbing in a garbage can."

"You will if you want to come to a Stoops meeting."

Sully tugged at his hat again. "Why are shoes in a garbage can? Who's Grace?"

"Some girl," I said, because I really didn't want to go into it.

"Don't be rude, Josie," said Lucy, frowning. "I like her."

Her tone stung. "I didn't say I *didn't* like her."

"Well, you weren't very welcoming! It was totally embarrassing. You didn't even ask about where she's from."

"I didn't need to! You were the one doing all the asking!" I snapped. Lucy kicked at a patch of grass, and an awkward silence hung in the air.

Finally, Lucy stomped off toward the garbage can and pulled out the dirty Vans. "I'll wash them, then," she said. "I don't want Grace to be mad at me. She actually *likes* the same things I do!"

I froze, staring at her. "What's that supposed to mean?"

I noticed Lucy roll her eyes before she turned her back toward me. "Never mind," she muttered.

"Stop fighting already," whined Amelia. "You two sound like Ellen and Sarah."

"Fine. We'll have a meeting now. But I need to tell Mom and Dad." I blinked back tears, not sure what Lucy and I sounded like anymore. We definitely didn't sound like best friends. "And I'll wash Grace's shoes," I added, taking them from Lucy's hands. I had to get out of here before I started crying. "I'll be back."

I didn't even bother asking Amelia to come home with me and Lucky the puppy. Lucy started asking her about soccer camp, and I bolted over to our townhouse. I threw Grace's pee-soaked shoe and its clean twin in the handwash cycle of the washing machine, told my parents where we were, and a few minutes later I was holding seven thin, red leashes, with puppies tugging me every which way.

"SURRRRRPRISE!" Amelia said as I walked up to where Lucy, Sully, Carlos, and Fernanda were now sitting. The puppies had just woken up from a nap, so they were really hyper. They jumped up on my friends' legs and sniffed at the potted plants. Tugger lunged for Carlos, who was sitting on a step, and tried to snatch his phone right from his hands.

"Awww!" said Fernanada. "They're so little!"

"Whoa!" said Carlos, grinning. "No way, little guy! Or girl? I don't need teeth marks on my new case. No bite! HEY, I SAID NO BITE!"

Amelia giggled. "Tugger's teeth are sharp like a T. rex. But Josie said they're only playing when they use their mouths. They're not going to hurt you or anything."

"We've held puppies before, Millie," said Lucy.

Her tone made me rise to my sister's defense, even though she was being such a whiner today. "Millie's just being helpful," I snapped before I could hold back the words.

Lucy opened her mouth to say something, but Fernanda lifted up a puppy and cooed, "Awww, hey, little pup! You're so cute! If I had your sharp teeth, I'd bite my brother's ugly phone case, too."

"It's not ugly," Carlos said, spinning it around for the rest of us as if he was doing a class presentation. "It's modern." Bright, bold, colorful swooshes splattered across the plastic, like an abstract painting you'd see at a museum. I agreed with him, actually. His case was pretty cool.

"It's splotches, is what it is." Fernanda put down Tugger and reached for another puppy, who was sniffing her feet. "I probably permanently smell like chlorine after this summer. Ha! Aw, this one's so big! And listen to that bark!"

"Yeah, she's the loudest one. Strongest, too, I think," I said. "I've been calling her Babbles. She's kinda an alpha dog."

"Alpha dog." Fernanda straightened her shoulders. "Sounds like me. I like that."

"What's an alpha dog?" asked Amelia.

"Leader of the pack," I explained. I glanced at Lucy, who was being unusually quiet, and tried to erase the fact I was annoyed with her. "Want to hold a puppy, Luce?" I asked her. She nodded and kneeled down beside Rocky, picking him up and letting him snuggle against her neck.

"Where'd all these puppies come from, Josie?" asked

Sully, tapping his pencil on a page in his detective notebook. My stomach fluttered. *Sully actually directed a question toward me!* I explained to my friends about how they were abandoned at the clinic, and that we were fostering them for two weeks.

"Speaking of owners," I continued, "you all did such an awesome job helping with Operation Home for Hamlet that I'm wondering if you'll help me get these puppies adopted to forever homes, too?"

Sully spun the notebook to a fresh sheet of paper. "A new case," he said, his eyes lighting up.

"Exactly." I matched his grin. "Whoa, whoa, hang on, Speedy!"

The fastest puppy of the litter tried to bolt after a squirrel that ran up a tree. I tugged her back, laughing.

"Speedy's my favorite," gushed Amelia. "Can I hold her, Josie?"

"Sure. But hold on real tight to that leash."

"I will," Amelia promised.

"So what do we call our new case?" asked Sully. "Operation Puppy Problems?"

"Awww, they're not *problems*," protested Amelia.

"The problem is that we need to find them each a great forever home, and we only have two weeks to do it," I said.

"Sounds like *no* problem to me," said Carlos, ruffling Houdini's fluffy head. "We're basically experts at animal adoptions now."

I snapped my fingers. "We need to do something different this time. Puppies require a very different strategy than pigs."

"Hmm." Sully chewed on his pencil.

"We need to do something . . . faster," I continued. "We've only got two weeks. So I was thinking, what if we organized an Adoptathon?"

"Great idea!" said Lucy. I beamed.

"Legal *and* adorable," added Fernanda.

Carlos scratched Lucky's head. "I'd adopt this one."

I felt my palms go clammy, and Amelia said in a singsongy voice, "Ohhhhhh, no way! That one's Josie's favorite!"

"Yeah, but . . ." I swallowed hard. All the puppies had to find good homes, because Mom and Dad were definitely not letting me keep one. I couldn't get attached to any of them, even though my sister was right. Lucky was my favorite of the litter. I loved the copper penny markings above her eyes, and the way she watched out for her brothers and sisters. It was like she was a leader and invisible, all at the same time, which was a confusing place to be in a big family. I could totally relate.

Besides, it'd be cool to have my favorite puppy be adopted by my friends. Then I could hang out with her all the time! Even though I might feel a *little* jealous that she wasn't mine.

"Lucky's cute, but she's a little . . . mild, don't you think? I like the strong girls. Awwww. I wish I could have a puppy sitting on my lap while I work on my coding." Fernanda lifted Babbles back up in her arms and nuzzled her nose to nose. "You want to code with me? Do ya? Do ya? See? She licked me! That means *yes* in dogspeak."

Carlos laughed. "NO. MORE. GIRLS. IN. OUR. HOUSE."

Fernanda rolled her eyes. "Whatever. There's no chance Mom will let us keep a puppy anyway, Los. It's just wishful thinking."

"Yeah, for me, too." I clapped my hands together. "Keep us posted though, after you talk to your mom."

"Twins equal *maybe*," Sully said slowly as he scribbled in the Case File.

"More like a big fat *no*. With a sad face emoji," clarified Fernanda.

"Okay," I said, thinking it through. "We can probably get one or two families from the vet's office. I'm sure there's someone out there looking to adopt a great dog. I'll talk with Dr. Stern when she gets back from her conference. Also, my parents suggested we charge a fifty-dollar adoption fee. That'll help cover the cost for their food, supplies, and vaccinations."

"So there're going to be four or five puppies that need some added marketing," said Lucy, scrunching her face up in thought.

"The adoption fliers worked well last time," I said. "Let's do that again but this time advertising the Adopt-athon. We'll hang them up in the usual spots—library, YMCA, vet's office, utility poles, maybe your parents have coworkers or friends or family who would be interested?"

"I'll design the fliers," said Carlos, tapping his flip-flops on the steps. I imagined all the cute art he could do for them. I bet he was really good at drawing puppies.

"I'll create the website," added Fernanda.

"You don't have time to make a website," shot back Carlos. "Your schedule is so busy already."

"What's wrong with that? I like to keep busy." She

shrugged. "I can do it, Josie. You can count on me."

"And we need a group pic of the litter," said Lucy, pulling out her cell phone.

"Good idea!" said Sully, nodding.

"But first, a group selfie!"

The whole Three Stoops crew positioned the puppies in a group on the steps, like they were taking a classroom photo. Amelia gave Lucy bunny ears, while Carlos stuck out his tongue and Fernanda raised her hands high in the air. We couldn't stop cracking up, and my stomach muscles began to ache from laughing so hard.

"Individual pics next," Fernanda said. "I'll create an online profile for each puppy. We can include their name, gender, and info about their personality."

"Perfect!" I said. "Can you create an online questionnaire, so people can apply right through the website? We've got to make sure they're the perfect match for the puppy. I'll help come up with the questions. We have some fliers at the vet's office on pet adoption."

"Oh yeah, that'd be easy to upload." Fernanda nodded. Lucy took a few steps closer to the puppies, snapping photos from high and low angles like a professional photographer.

Sully scribbled down notes as fast as he could while Amelia, Lucy, and I told him about all the puppies and their personalities so far. My little sister gently puppeteered Speedy's paws across the brick step, as if she was a puppy playing the piano, and Lucy held out her phone, videoing the scene and laughing.

"Okay, guys," Sully said, turning to a blank page. "I think we've got a good plan here."

"Me too." I nodded. "I've gotta put the puppies back now and get to the pet store before it's dark."

"Right." Lucy put her phone away. "But we have one more case to go over first." I scowled. I was running out of time to get to the pet store, and Lucy sure was being bossy today! "It's the Case of the New Neighbor," she continued. "Her name's Grace, and she's our age. Well, she's technically thirteen, but she's in our grade in school."

"We have a new neighbor?" gasped Fernanda. "Spill the deets!"

Sully wrote down the Case of the New Neighbor at the top of the page and started taking notes.

Lucy told our friends about how Grace and her family had moved here from California, that they were staying nearby in temporary housing, how Grace was into music and trying to get "discovered" with her "EP," and how they were moving into Mrs. Taglioni's townhouse even though we didn't even know it was up for sale, and then finally, the terrible incident with Lucky peeing on her shoes.

But Lucy was my best friend through and through, and all I really heard was *blah blah blah Grace is so cool and amazing blah blah blah*. Maybe I was a little bit jealous.

"Ew," said Fernanda, wrinkling her nose over Lucky and the Vans fiasco. "That was definitely *un*lucky." She set Blue down on the stoop and wagged a finger at her. "You'd better not pee on me!"

"Anyway, Grace is pretty mad," said Lucy.

"It's not a case," I said, not meeting Lucy's eyes. "It's just a new neighbor. It's no big deal."

"What?" Fernanda looked at me with wide eyes. "It's a *huge* deal, Josie! When's the last time someone our age moved into our neighborhood? I can't even remember, it's been that long. So, Lucy, when is Grace moving in?"

"Dunno. She said soon, though. Anyway, Sully, that's all the intel on that," said Lucy. "It's going to take some work to make her one of our crew." Her face lit up suddenly. "Oh! Maybe she'd want a puppy? I wonder if she has a dog already."

"Um." I wrinkled my nose. "If Grace doesn't like puppy pee on her shoes, I'm pretty sure she doesn't have a dog."

What I didn't say out loud: *That girl is not adopting one of my dogs!*

"Okay, so maybe she's not a dog person . . . ," Lucy agreed. "Hmm. I wonder if purple eye shadow is popular in California."

"Her eye shadow was *so* pretty!" chimed in Amelia.

The last thing I wanted to talk about was the Case of the New Neighbor let alone solve a problem I didn't want to be involved in. I made a face. If Lucy could call a Three Stoops meeting about things that had to do with *me*—two things, actually—then I could call an end to the meeting whenever I wanted.

"Time to put the dogs back and run to the store, Millie," I said, and my little sister clapped her hands happily. I shook the leashes, motioning for any puppies being held to be returned to the ground. "Thanks, guys," I said. "I think the Adoptathon is going to be amazing! We've gotta run. Talk later?"

We all said goodbye. I led the puppies around to the

back alley behind our townhouses, feeling better already with a bit more space between Lucy and me. Amelia zipped ahead, kicking an invisible soccer ball down the block.

The clumsy, curious puppies bounded at my side, making me laugh.

Yeah, definitely better.

Sometimes when people are too much to deal with, a girl just needs a dog pack.

Chapter 10

TURN OF EVENTS

As soon as the puppies heard my feet on the stairs, they started barking inside the crate and tumbling over each other. These wigglers sure were ready for a walk! I had read in one of my puppy guides about how important it was to exercise your dog first thing in the morning.

"Hiya, puppies!" I unlocked the door to the crate. They bolted across the living room and jumped on the couch. They tried to climb up my legs and scratched my shins. They yelped and sniffed and jumped. "Hang on, hang on! I need to grab your leashes!"

I stepped in a surprise puddle on the floor. How did *that* happen so fast? Ugh! I quickly cleaned it up with paper towels and took the dogs on walks in two groups.

My forehead already glistened with sweat from the humid July air.

Cars whooshed down the street. A mom pushing a baby stroller on the sidewalk offered me a "Morning!" and a little wave. Two puppies scampered alongside Sugar and me, who actually seemed to like the company even though she was a total slowpoke.

That's when I saw it and stopped in my tracks. There had been loads of Under Contract signs over the years on our block, but never, ever next door at Mrs. Taglioni's. It had appeared on her front window, the way flowers bloom on our dogwood tree: sudden, overnight, and without telling us.

I felt my spirits deflate. So it was true about Grace moving in. I had hoped that was all some mix-up, like maybe she got her address confused. Ugh. Wishful thinking.

Mrs. Taglioni had been my next-door neighbor my whole life. She'd lived in that townhouse for decades, probably. Sure, we hadn't always gotten along. But things were different now—weren't they? She was like my wise old grandmother, just one door down. We had lemonade on her front stoop. I helped her plant her bulbs. I bought her chamomile tea sometimes with my allowance money. And, most importantly, we visited Hamlet together every month.

Like, *last weekend*.

I shook my head in disbelief. We spent all day Saturday together. How could she not mention anything about this? Then another horrible thought struck me. Was Mrs. Taglioni moving away because of *us*? Were we so loud and chaotic that living next door to us was too stressful? I felt my mouth go dry. I thought we were friends now. Maybe I'd been wrong?

I sighed. It seemed like I didn't understand any of my friends anymore.

I rubbed Sugar's soft golden neck, staring at the Under Contract sign, and whispered, "There's just no *way*."

It might as well be an alien invasion, that's how strange it felt to see such a thing.

Sugar leaned against my leg, and she whimpered, making the puppies perk their ears. "Yeah," I said. "That's how I feel right now, too. C'mon, let's go inside."

She wobbled on the steps getting back into the townhouse, but I helped steady her legs. It was only eight a.m., but it felt like half the day had passed. Inside, we were met with an explosion of chaos that made me temporarily forget about the Case of the New Neighbor.

"Where's my other shin guard?" yelled Amelia, digging through the hall closet. She popped her head out and glared at me.

"Don't look at me. *I'm* not wearing them," I said defensively, taking off my sandals and unclipping Sugar's leash from her leather collar. Her dog tags jingled as she gave her neck a shake and slowly padded to the living room, where she dropped onto the wood floor and stretched her body out.

"Ugh!" Amelia sighed and went back to digging through the mound of shoes and socks, tossing a football out of the way and into the hall. "It's not fair you get to walk them and I gotta go to soccer camp!"

"Millie, you loved soccer camp last week. Let's take the whining down a notch, okay?" said Mom gently. "Here. I'll help you find that missing shin guard. . . ." I unclipped the leashes from the puppies' collars, and they bolted across the living room. "Josie, did the dogs go out?"

"Yes, Mom." I rolled my eyes. "I literally just walked in."

"—But that's my shirt!" Sarah yelled, her voice carrying from upstairs.

"You said I could borrow it!" Ellen was yelling back.

"That was LAST WEEK!"

"Ladies! Ladies! Let's remember there are more important things in life than clothes." I heard Dad clapping his hands, like he didn't know what else to do to break up a wardrobe argument. "I just can't believe it about Molly," he said as he walked down the stairs, as if he was resuming a conversation with my mom that had been on pause.

Mom stood in the foyer in a bathrobe, drinking a mug of steaming black coffee. "Me either," she said, shaking her head. "I never thought this day would come."

I paused in the doorway, watching my parents move toward the back door that led to the yard. Maybe I would overhear some new intel, like a good reason for why Mrs. Taglioni was moving out of the neighborhood. After the puppies had a chance to drink fresh water, I let them follow me into the fenced backyard.

"Hey, Mom, hey, Dad," I said.

"Hi, sweetie," Mom said. "What time do you head to Eastside?"

"Leaving in about an hour," I said, yawning. I'd stayed up late last night reading a book by a famous dog behaviorist named Cesar Millan. I'd learned about how to be a calm and assertive pack leader, and why exercise was extremely important for keeping a dog emotionally and physically balanced. "Dr. Stern is back today," I continued.

Dad stopped his pacing and pulled out a patio chair. Taking a seat, he gazed next door at Mrs. Taglioni's place. "Remember the first time we met her, Emily, right after we closed on our house?"

"Of course I remember," said Mom with a laugh. "I was three days overdue with Tom. I could barely walk up the steps!"

I had never heard this story before. "Tell me what happened," I said, smiling.

"Well," Mom said, "we loved this little townhouse, but it needed a lot of work. We didn't have the money to pay contractors, so we had to DIY most projects. I was so pregnant I couldn't really help out until after Tom was born. So, anyway, your dad had this bright idea to tear down the drywall in the upstairs bathroom, the day after we moved in! Now, this was before we added insulation in the shared wall, so you can imagine how Mrs. Taglioni felt about these new neighbors of hers *making a racket* next door. . . ."

"Yeah, she probably wasn't happy about that at all." I laughed, remembering how she used to complain at the smallest noise. I liked to think she had grown fond of our noises now that we were all friends. But maybe I'd been wrong about that.

"She came banging on the front door right then and there! But once she saw how pregnant I was, she settled down." Mom winked. "She even knit baby Tom a hat."

"It just doesn't seem right," Dad said, sighing. "Molly not living next door . . . What did she say when you talked to her?"

"Well, she said that it's a big place for one woman to live in all alone, and she'd been thinking about selling for a while now. She met with a few real estate agents, and they thought the market was strong. And before the agent posted the listing to the public, this great offer came in that she couldn't refuse—quick close and everything."

"I wish . . . Mrs. Taglioni would've told me," I admitted, sitting down in the chair next to my dad. "It feels like . . . I don't know . . . like she did it behind my back."

"Oh, sweetie. I know it's a bit shocking, but Mrs.

Taglioni is doing what she thinks is best for her—and her brother." Mom patted my hand. Her palm was warm from gripping her coffee mug.

"What's Mr. Upton got to do with this?"

"Oh! You didn't hear? She's moving to the farm."

My eyes widened. *"Really?"*

Dad unfolded his morning newspaper. "Josie, maybe she was afraid she'd upset you with the news? I know how mature you are, but twelve might seem very young to someone like Mrs. Taglioni. And she must know how attached you've become to her."

I blew a stray hair from my face. "Yeah. Maybe."

"Just go bang on her door and ask her what's going on," added Dad with a laugh. "And if she complains about the banging, just tell her it's payback for all the years she's done it to us!"

"Stephen, you're terrible." Mom chuckled. "Josie, do not listen to your father. Just bring it up next time you see her if it feels natural to you. I'm sure she'll be happy to talk to you about it. Then you can hear more about what her life will be like on the farm."

A tight pressure released from my chest, and I could expand my lungs a little easier now. "Hamlet will love having more people around," I said. "And Mrs. Taglioni makes her the best corn bread. Hamlet wags her long, hairy pig tail every time she sees her."

"Do pigs wag their tails?" Dad asked. "I didn't notice that with Hamlet."

"They sort of whisk them back and forth, like cows," I explained.

Mom continued to me, "Now, Josie, I know how much Mr. Upton and Mrs. Taglioni love having you and Lucy visit the farm, so we'll figure out a way for you to continue your visits." She shielded her face from the sun with her hand. "Maybe the whole family could go together next month? I'd love to see Hamlet again, especially if she's as big as you say she is!"

"Oh, she's *huge*, Mom. A total dinosaur pig! Wait until you see her." I grinned. Maybe Mrs. Taglioni moving away wouldn't be such a terrible thing. The farm could be like my second home. Maybe I'd get to visit more often, too—with or without Lucy.

But still, I'd miss having Mrs. Taglioni next door.

And whether I liked it or not, I had to figure out how to solve the Case of the New Neighbor problem.

I sighed, my eyes trailing across our little yard until my gaze settled on Sugar. She was stretched out on a small patch of grass near the fence. I hadn't realized that she had snuck out the back door when we came out; I had thought she was sleeping in the living room. Then I noticed something strange. Her body was shaking! No, not shaking—convulsing. A bolt of fear shot down my spine.

"Mom! Dad!" I raced down the steps into the small, grassy area. I leaned next to Sugar and gently pressed my palm against her fur, right above her heart.

"What's wrong, Josie?"

Thump, thump. Thump, thump.

It was beating so fast!

"It's Sugar!" I yelled. "Something's wrong!"

Mom raced over to our dog's side. "Oh my gosh. . . . Stephen, come here! I think Sugar's having a seizure."

Sugar's body stopped shaking, and her chest slowly rose and fell with each labored breath. Relief washed over me. Whatever had just happened was over, and she was still breathing. My muscles relaxed. I stroked Sugar's soft golden-blond fur. I didn't really know what a seizure was, but whatever I'd witnessed was definitely *not* normal. I'd never seen her body shake like that.

"Something's wrong with her," I said, trying not to cry. Suddenly I felt a sense of urgency like I had never felt before. I pressed my fingers more firmly on Sugar's stomach and chest, across the hard edges of ribs, and along her spine, and sharper, protruding hipbones, like I'd learned from Dr. Stern countless times during her dog examinations. "Sugar feels really skinny, too. Has she lost a lot of weight?"

Mom reached for her cell phone. "She hasn't had much of an appetite lately, but she had a clear health report at her last checkup. I'm calling Cassandra."

Sugar closed her eyes as I stroked her soft fur. All these months I'd been hanging out at Eastside Veterinary Clinic, helping care for other people's pets, when something was wrong with my own dog right before my eyes. And I'd never noticed it, not until now. I blinked back the tears.

Mom raised the phone to her ear and said, "Cassandra? Hi. Yes, the puppies are fine—Josie's taking great care of them. Actually, this is about Sugar. I wonder, is there any chance you have a few minutes open this morning? We think she just had a seizure, and—yes, she was shaking, but it was more than a tremble. Josie thinks she's lost a lot of weight, and she's been more tired than normal. Oh, thank you so much! We'll come right now. Thank you. See you soon."

Mom hung up the call and got to her feet.

"She's squeezing us in. Stephen, can you get the van—it's parked on the street down by the church? Wait, no, the clinic is only a few blocks away—let's just grab a cab, Josie. Hurry! I'll get my purse."

I patted Sugar gently and whispered, "It'll be okay, girl. We'll get you checked out."

Her ears twitched as she struggled to sit up. She was panting, but her eyes had that dreamy half-closed look to them, like they get when she's sunbathing. She seemed stable, but still. Seeing her shake like that was scary. I kept my hands close to her body, just in case she needed help being steady on her feet.

"Hang on! The puppies!" Dad said, reaching for Babbles, who was barking at a potted plant. "You stay with Sugar, Josie. Your mom and I will put the puppies back in the crate." He stopped and slapped his forehead. "Oh no—I have our department meeting at ten. I can't go to the clinic and make it on time. I'm so sorry. Will you two be okay with Sugar at the clinic without me?"

Mom scooped Speedy into her arms. "We'll be fine. Let's hurry and get these puppies secured away." My parents gathered the squirming puppies and finagled them back into the crate. I hugged Sugar and kissed the top of her head while we waited.

"I'm right here, girl," I whispered into her ear. "Right here."

I was trying to calm down Sugar, but part of me hoped the words would calm me down, too.

Chapter 11

ADOPT, DON'T SHOP

Sugar tucked her tail between her legs as she stood in the examination room. Dogs can't talk the way humans can, but they use their bodies to communicate how they feel. A tail between her legs meant Sugar was nervous. But that was normal. Most animals felt anxious when they visited the clinic, no matter how gentle and experienced Dr. Stern was. Many of her patients had known her for years! Animals relied on instinct in order to survive, and that was stronger than anything else.

I felt my throat clench up as Dr. Stern slowly stroked Sugar's fur. She listened to her heartbeat and tenderly pressed into her abdomen with her hands. Daniel took notes in the corner.

"Well," Dr. Stern said finally, "I'm not feeling a mass or tumor, but we'll need diagnostic testing to learn more about what's going on inside Sugar's body. She has lost quite a bit of weight since her last visit, and that seizure is concerning. Tell me more about what happened this morning."

"We were out back, and I looked over and her whole body was just . . . *convulsing*," I explained. "It only lasted a few seconds, maybe? She didn't seem to be in any pain afterward, but it was scary."

"Has that ever happened before?"

"Not that we've seen," said Mom. "But I'll double-check with all the kids. I'm positive they would've mentioned it though."

"Have you noticed anything else unusual with Sugar's behavior recently?"

"She's been really tired lately," I said. "And she's not as steady on her feet. On stairs, especially. She's wobbly."

"Most of the time she just sleeps on the first floor because the stairs are too difficult for her now," added Mom. "But she's always liked to nap. Sugar hasn't been particularly high energy for years."

"I have to *really* jingle her leash for her to come to the

door," I said. "But that's normal for senior dogs, right?"

Dr. Stern continued to pet Sugar's head as she listened to us. "Anything else?"

"Well." I bit the inside of my cheek. "She had an accident in the living room a few days ago."

"She did?" Mom turned her head. "Sugar is usually very good with bladder control."

My gaze lowered to the tiled floor. "I didn't say anything because I thought it was one of the puppies at first."

"Oh, honey. It's okay." I felt Mom's reassuring hands close around my shoulders. "But now that you mention it, Cassandra, Sugar has been barking a lot lately. She's never been a barking type of dog. I didn't think anything of it until now."

"Any signs of aggression?"

We shook our heads. "Never," said Mom.

"Confusion?"

"No. At least, I don't think so?" I leaned against the cabinets along the wall, thinking. "Wait! When I was walking her around the block the other day, she had this moment when, I don't know, she seemed lost? Like she didn't know how to get home."

Dr. Stern got to her feet and jotted notes down in

Sugar's chart. "You're going to need to take Sugar to a specialist downtown, but while you're here in the office, I recommend we take a chest X-ray. I have back-to-back patients this morning, but Daniel can do this for you on-site now and I'll call you in a bit with the results." She turned to Daniel, tapping her chin with a finger. "Let's do some blood work, too. And Josie, I understand if you don't want to stay and help out this morning. You're welcome to go home if you'd like."

I bit my lip. I wasn't sure what I wanted to do.

"Does Sugar need to stay for the day, or should I just wait?" asked Mom.

"You can wait. It will only take a few minutes."

"Why do you need her blood?" I added.

"It will give us more information," explained Dr. Stern. "We want to make sure it's not a toxin or liver failure or something else we can't see that's causing Sugar's symptoms." Dr. Stern nodded to Daniel, and he reached for Sugar's leash. "Monitor her closely today, and let me know if there are any changes in her behavior."

"We will," I said. "And Dr. Stern? Would it be okay if I watched Daniel do the X-ray? I won't get in his way, I promise."

She offered me a kind smile. "I wish I could allow

that, Josie, but it's illegal for anyone under eighteen to be in a radiation room. It'll only be a few minutes, and she'll be in excellent hands. You can show your mom around the waiting room, explain what you do here. Maybe feed the Kingdom? I haven't had a chance yet this morning."

Mom squinted her eyes. "Kingdom?"

"Lou's name for the lobby aquarium," I said.

"Oh, I *love* aquariums!" Mom's voice was suspiciously chipper. I rolled my eyes. Sugar being sick was serious. I didn't need her to baby me.

I watched as Daniel led Sugar down the hallway and into another room. "It won't hurt, Sugar! Be a good girl!" I called out after her. If she could be brave, I would be brave, too.

"Thank you, Cassandra," said Mom, trailing behind me. "For squeezing us in. I know how busy you are."

"Happy to help. You know how much I adore Sugar. Miss Janice can help you with your bill, and I'll be in touch very soon regarding results and next steps. Also we're going to put Sugar on an antiseizure medication. Now, if she has another seizure, take her here immediately." Dr. Stern handed Mom a business card I recognized as coming from the emergency animal hospital downtown. We kept a stack of those cards at the front desk, and there was one taped to the glass window of the clinic, too.

By the time I took care of the Kingdom and helped Miss Janice stack bags of dog food on the shelves in the lobby, Daniel was finished with the X-rays and blood tests. Sugar seemed to be back to her old self, so Mom and I walked home slowly with her, letting her take lots of sniffing and potty breaks.

We passed Fernanda, who was sitting on her stoop. "Hey! And hi, Mrs. Shilling!" she said, looking up from her phone. "We're going swimming at the Y tomorrow for open swim—want to come? You don't have to be on a swim team or anything."

"Hi, Fernanda! Here, I'll put Sugar back, Josie," said Mom, taking the leash from my hands. "Just come inside when you're ready."

When I sat down, Fernanda was nearly bursting with excitement. Which was fine by me, because I wasn't ready to share about Sugar's seizure quite yet.

"Everyone is coming! Finally, the Three Stoops crew hangs at my pool. I've been, like, waiting all summer for you guys to come! I can't handle my swim team friends anymore. We'll take the one-p.m. bus, okay?"

The door slammed shut behind her, and Carlos

appeared. "You're complaining about your swimming friends again? They aren't that bad."

Fernanda rolled her eyes. "Yeah, they are. It's not even fun to be around them anymore."

"Then hang out with my swim friends," Carlos said. "Or get new ones."

"I don't need *new* ones. I have *you* guys." Fernanda set her phone down on the top step. "So, you're coming tomorrow, right, Josie?"

Confusing thoughts swirled in my mind. Fernanda was right. We hadn't all been to the city YMCA pool together yet this summer, and last summer we went all the time. But as much fun as it sounded like it would be, I needed to watch the puppies and keep an eye on Sugar in case she had another seizure. "I'm not sure if I can," I said slowly. "Let me get back to you, okay?"

Fernanda nodded, and Carlos gave her a sly smile. "Did you tell her?" he asked. Fernanda shook her head.

My heart beat a little faster. "Tell me what?"

"Mom said YES!"

"Yes about what?"

"Adopting a puppy!"

"NO WAY!"

"Yep!" Fernanda grinned. "She wants to talk to Dr.

Stern though and just make sure they're all healthy."

"They're healthy. I can promise you that." I bounced up on my toes. "I'm even crate training them." I whooped out loud. "This is awesome news! I'm SO excited! Which one do you want, do you think?"

"Babbles," Fernanda said right as Carlos replied, "Tugger."

"Wait." Carlos pointed his ballpoint pen at his sister. "Josie said that one was the alpha. She's going to be hard to train, if she always thinks she's in charge."

Fernanda narrowed her eyes. "Josie said Babbles needed a strong personality to be the alpha dog over her. That's exactly why we should adopt her. She'll listen to me. Babbles can't go to some home where the owner is a pushover, right, Josie? Hello, PROBLEMS!"

"Fernanda has a point," I agreed. "That's when dogs can start showing negative behaviors, like aggression and dominance."

"But Tugger's so playful," Carlos protested. He stomped his sneakers on a brick step and turned them sideways, admiring his ink sketches along the rubber trim. Then he gave Fernanda a sideways grin, the big kind that revealed his mouth full of braces. He'd just got them a few months ago, and since then, he didn't smile that big often. "So it's decided!"

"No, it's not." She crossed her arms over her chest.

"You guys just need to see the puppies again—then you'll be able to decide," I said. "Fernanda, how's the website coming along?"

"Amaaaazing. Lucy's photos are awesome. Wait until you see this—" She opened up a web browser on her phone, tapped "www.dogdaysinthecity.com," and handed it to me.

"Wow," I breathed as the website loaded. "Dog Days Adoptathon—that's so perfect! I can't believe how fast you guys pulled this together." Lucy's photos were really beautiful, and the twins did a great job with the website layout and design elements. I scrolled down the webpage, where a big photo of the entire litter of puppies was the backdrop image, and the text below read *Adopt, Don't Shop!* in Carlos's calligraphy. All the puppies' names were listed on the homepage, and when you ran the cursor over each puppy name and photo, it glowed in a different color and would link you to a bio page on that individual puppy. There was also an email icon so that potential adopters could contact me.

Reading over each description, I laughed, glancing at

Fernanda. "You guys edited my descriptions of the puppies. Houdini has puzzle-solving skills?!"

She grinned. "Lucy didn't think writing 'Escape Artist' would be a positive puppy trait."

"Oh, and the adoption application questions! You guys added a few to my suggestions. . . . *Are there any known pet allergies in the family? Is everyone in the household in agreement with adopting a pet? Number of hours the dog will be alone during the day?* These are all perfect." I handed the phone back to Fernanda. "All right, so you guys just need to pick your puppy, and then we can add an *ADOPTED!* stamp over that dog's picture."

Fernanda leaned back on her palms. "Oh, it's decided."

Carlos rolled his eyes. "Nope. And Mom said it has to be a mutual decision."

"So, make it mutual, Los!"

"We only have ten days left before the Adoptathon," I reminded them. "You have until then to get first pick of the litter!"

"Wait." Carlos spun the ballpoint pen tucked behind his ear, considering. "Do we have to fill out an adoption application?"

"Nah. You're approved." I laughed. "But the puppy

will cost you a fifty-dollar adoption fee."

Something tugged at my heart, but I couldn't quite place the confusing emotion. The smile on my face melted away. It's strange how sad and happy things can happen on the same day.

Chapter 12

FAMILY MATTERS

My siblings gathered in the living room. We flopped over the couch armrests, splayed out on the carpet, and leaned back in the old worn recliner while Mom and Dad settled into the couch. From the looks on my family's faces, it was clear everyone had learned about Sugar's seizure.

It was almost dinnertime, but most of the puppies were in the crate, except for Speedy in Amelia's arms and Lucky curled up at Sugar's paws. "Hiya, Lucky!" I said, clapping my hands. She came bounding toward me to give me puppy kisses.

"Fiiiiiine," said Tom, setting down his fantasy football magazine. "Hand one over."

"Hand what over?"

"A puppy."

I grinned. "Really?"

"I feel bad for the ones stuck in the crate." He shook his head. "Like second-string puppies."

"Of course you would use a football analogy," commented Ellen.

"Well, amiright or amiright? Second- and *third*-string puppies. Waiting on the bench. Howling for attention . . ."

"Yeah, Babbles IS howling, Josie!" agreed Amelia.

"Tom, you're so dramatic." But even Ellen cracked a smile. "Okay. Josie, hand me a puppy, too."

I grinned. I handed Tom the little climber, Rocky, because I figured he'd like wrestling with him, and then passed Houdini over to Ellen. She'd keep a close watch on him and make sure he didn't get away. That curious little puppy was always disappearing under the couch, or trying to go up the stairs, or napping behind the curtain.

Sarah stretched her arms out. "Well, that's not fair. If everyone gets to hold a puppy, I want to hold one, too." She motioned grabby hands at me.

"Really?" I couldn't mask the surprise in my voice.

"Don't make me change my mind."

I laughed. "Okay! Here's Babbles. She's another girl.

Super strong, probably the leader of the litter. . . . She's got, um, opinions. I think you'll get along. And she's Fernanda's favorite!" I handed Babbles to my sister, and she yelped loudly in Sarah's face. Sarah couldn't help but smile as she pulled the puppy close, shushing her. I knew it! Holding a cute puppy could melt anyone's heart—even a teenager with an attitude problem.

I looked around the room and felt a warm sensation spread from my heart throughout my chest. "Two left." I clapped my hands together. "Mom, Dad? Tugger and Blue need human friends!"

Mom smiled. "Hand me Blue." Then she shot Dad a pointed look. "Honey, Tugger is waiting."

Dad paused, his lips pursing together. "Fine. Josie, hand me Tugger."

I giggled. "It's not *Tigger*, Dad. It's Tugger."

I set Tugger in Dad's lap. He stared at him for a second and then finally petted Tugger's furry head. "Okay, kids, let's start the family meeting." Dad took a deep breath. "Everyone ready?"

I tenderly curled up next to Sugar on the carpet, careful not to put any pressure on her body, and placed Lucky in between us so she could share my puppy snuggles, too. The only thing that could have made this family meeting better was if Sugar was healthy and Hamlet was here, like last winter.

Mom stroked Blue's back. Her eyes slowly closed. "Dr. Stern called a few minutes ago," Mom began. "Sugar's chest X-ray was clear, but she sent the files to a specialist downtown. We need to take Sugar there for an MRI. I've already called and they squeezed us in tomorrow, because of the seriousness of Sugar's symptoms.

"Sugar's on an antiseizure medication, but tonight and tomorrow morning, we all need to keep an eye on her, and let me know *immediately* if you notice anything unusual or if she has another seizure. Dr. Stern said it might take time for the medicine to start working."

Lucky sniffed at Sugar, trying to wiggle against her belly. Sugar nudged her away with her nose, making Lucky start to whine. I pulled the puppy closer to me.

"Give her some space, Lucky," I said. Then I glanced at my parents. "So that's all we know until the MRI?"

Mom and Dad exchanged a look. Mom's chin trembled, the way it does when she's about to cry, which doesn't happen that often. "Sugar's old, sweetie," Dad said, his voice breaking. "I just want us all to be emotionally prepared."

"Emotionally prepared for what?" Amelia crossed her arms in her lap. She blinked, glancing around at my siblings' blank expressions.

"You're kidding, right, Squirt?" said Sarah. Her expression transformed from annoyance into a fuming glare when she looked at my parents. I felt my nerves flare. How could she be so cruel, especially at a time like this?

"Sarah," snapped Ellen. "Millie's young and—"

"What?" Amelia's voice shook a little as she stared at Sarah. "What's going on?"

Mom took a deep breath.

"Tomorrow Dad and I will take Sugar to the appointment downtown," Mom said. "Dad is going to take a day off work. If any of you kids would like to come with us, you are welcome to, but I have a feeling there will be a lot of waiting around, and I know you all have important jobs and camp this summer."

Dad looked down at the puppy sleeping in his lap. "We just want you to know that there are a lot of unknowns right now," he said. "Sugar is very old, and she's had a wonderful, long life. . . ."

Sarah jumped to her feet, cradling her puppy close.

"Just say it, Dad," she exploded. "Just SAY IT! We might have to put Sugar down, is that it? Why don't you just come out and SAY IT?!"

"What?" Amelia's voice was small, like a little piece of puzzle trying to fit its way into a grown-up conversation.

"That's what happened last year to Nissa's dog," Sarah said, her eyes welling up. "Her parents sat her down and did this whole *blah-blah-blah* talk that the dog was sick, and then one day she went home after field hockey, and her parents said 'Oh hey, your dog died today!' DIED! They had put her down without even TALKING TO HER ABOUT IT!" Tears streamed down Sarah's face, and it hit me suddenly that I hadn't realized how much Sarah loved Sugar. After all, she grew up with her, too.

"Mom? Dad?" I asked, gently placing my hand over Sugar's warm chest. "You're not . . . going to do that, are you?"

"Absolutely not," Dad said firmly. He stood up and enveloped Sarah in a big hug. She melted against his shoulder, sobs taking over whatever muffled words she was trying to say. I felt tears welling up inside. "Sarah, that would never happen without talking to you all first—please don't worry." He gave her a big squeeze, and Sarah slowly nodded. "Don't worry. Right now it's just tests, okay? Sugar is hanging in there. She's being strong. We need to be strong, too."

"And it's natural to be upset," added Mom, making eye contact with each one of us. "Or feel confused about what's going to happen next. Sugar's been with us a long time, and she's a wonderful dog. There's a lot we don't know yet, so let's just take things one step at a time, okay? We're in this together as a family, just like your dad said. We promise."

Amelia snuggled up against Speedy. Dad set Tugger down on the floor next to Sugar and Lucky, and the puppy suddenly started rooting at Sugar's belly. Sugar let out a low growl, and Lucky erupted into startled howls.

"Whoa!" said Amelia, sitting up. "It's okay, Sugar! Why's she growling?"

A small smile crossed Mom's face. "She's just telling her to back off."

"Why?"

"Tugger's trying to nurse," explained Ellen. "Unsuccessfully, of course."

Tom made a face. "Gross."

"Awww!" Amelia cooed. "They miss their mommy."

"*And* they're hungry. I'll get their food ready. Sorry, Sugar!" I lifted the puppies away from Sugar's belly, and our golden retriever relaxed and closed her eyes. Then I paused, turning to look at my little sister. "Millie, want to help me?"

My little sister's eyes lit up. "YES!"

"Okay, c'mon!" I motioned her toward the kitchen, where we divided the puppy food portions equally into seven little bowls, and placed them on top of layered paper towels on the tile floor. Puppy feeding time sure was cute, but it was messy, too!

"Sarah?" Dad was saying as we reentered the living room. "You okay?"

"Yeah, Dad." She wiped her nose with the back of her hand. "But remember you promised."

"Don't worry." Dad gave her another hug and then clapped his hands, "Okay! Who wants pizza? I think pizza night sounds like a good idea to me."

"ME!" called Amelia as she lifted Speedy back into her arms. "Cheese, please!"

"I'm starving," said Tom. "I've been surviving on fine espresso all day."

Ellen laughed. "You're an espresso drinker now? Really?"

"Yes." Tom placed a hand over his heart, pretending

to be offended. "I'm a highly trained barista. What, you think I drink regular *drip* coffee?"

Sarah rolled her eyes, fingers curling into Babbles's soft puppy fur. "How are you always starving? Don't they feed you, like, bagels and croissants at the coffee shop?"

"I'm having a growth spurt," Tom said with a grin. "I need sustenance."

"Oh, please. Like pizza is sustenance." Sarah laughed, and it made me smile, too. Sarah had the strange ability to set the mood for our entire family. When she let her guard down, I relaxed. When she was angry and tense, I fed off that energy, too. Maybe Sarah had a bit of alpha dog in her, like Babbles. My sister might act like she was too cool for our family most of the time, but she was also hurting inside about Sugar. That was something we had in common.

"All right, c'mon, Millie. Can we feed them now? They're all wiggly and whining!"

"How long are they staying here again? They sure are a lot of work, aren't they," said Ellen.

"Oh, Ellen. The puppies are just a phase." My brother pointed toward his right ear and said dramatically, "Like the earring thing, remember? This too shall pass."

Tom had shown up last Thanksgiving with not only a squirming piglet but his ear pierced, too! But by March or so, he'd stopped wearing the earring.

"An earring is one thing," Dad said, chuckling. "And seven puppies are quite another. For starters, they poop."

"Well, Tom poops! And it totally stinks!" said Amelia, and Tom burst out laughing.

"So I have a healthy colon. That's nothing to be ashamed about."

"Remind me, when do you and your colon go back to college again?" asked Sarah, rolling her eyes, making Ellen laugh.

"All right, all right, let's move on, kids." Mom raised her palm in the air, like she drew the line at poop talk. "Let's not be gross. And Stephen! I want anchovies on my pizza!"

Tom pursed his lips into a funny expression and muttered to my sisters, "You know what's gross? Anchovies! YUCK!"

Mom playfully tossed a couch pillow at him. "Ha, ha," she deadpanned. "Now let's help feed these puppies while we're waiting on the pizza, okay kids?"

Later that night, Tom, Ellen, and Sarah all had plans

with their friends, and Amelia curled up on the couch next to me.

Amelia looked over, her eyes wide and hopeful. "Wanna watch a movie together?"

I smiled. Sometimes I felt like I was in-between. I wasn't old enough yet to go out after dinner with my friends, like my older siblings. But I still felt too old to hang out all the time with my little sister. But tonight, lounging around with Amelia, Sugar, and the puppies sounded like just what we both needed.

I moved to the floor, where Sugar was sleeping, and gently stroked her back. "What movie?"

"Maybe . . . *101 Dalmatians*?"

I smiled. "Sure, Millie. Let's bring the puppies over to watch, too!"

That night after the movie ended, my parents let us stay up late talking and snuggling with the black-and-brown puppies on the couch. Amelia and I shared all the things we loved about Sugar. Dad even brought us bowls of mint chocolate chip ice cream (which we had to keep away from the dogs, who all desperately wanted a sniff and a lick). It felt good not to worry about how I looked or acted, or whether I was cool enough. My family didn't care about those things—and right now, it felt like they were the only people in my life who didn't.

Sometimes when your heart is sad and your mind is worried, all you can do is hold a puppy close to your chest, laugh with your little sister, and wish for better days ahead.

Chapter 13

TIME WILL TELL

The waiting room at the specialist's office was packed wall-to-wall with pet owners and their sick animals. Sugar, who usually got along with other dogs, was being shy. She curled up on the shiny tile floor, right by my sandals, refusing to greet anyone. I gently brushed the fur along her neck with my toes. She leaned back onto my feet, snuggling close against my skin.

"Mom, I don't think Sugar wants to be here. She seems nervous. Scared, maybe. It smells funny in here."

My mom's gaze floated around the waiting room. "Well, I'm sure none of the animals want to be here, Josie, same as when people don't want to go to the hospital. But we're only here to help her. You know that better than anyone."

Mom was right. I did know that. We needed to make sure Sugar was healthy, and we couldn't do that without taking her to this specialist.

"When's Dad getting here?" I asked.

"Just a few minutes, sweetie. The parking garage is close by."

I cracked my knuckles, trying to calm my nerves. I wasn't sure if Sugar could smell or feel my fear, but I knew animals had strong instincts. They were pack animals. I was Sugar's leader, or at least one of them. If I was nervous, she'd be nervous. I stretched my arms high above my head, trying to release the tension pressing against my shoulder blades and back.

Better.

"It's okay, Sugar," I said softly, and then repeated it again. "It's gonna be okay."

"Sugar Shilling?"

A lady with glasses pressed open a door that led to a corridor. She clutched a manila folder close to her chest—Sugar's new-patient file, I figured—and I felt my hands start to sweat again.

"Yes! Here we are," said Mom, standing up. I gently led Sugar through the doorway, following the employee, who directed us into a standard-looking veterinary examination room that had a faint chemical smell lingering in the air.

"I'm Mia. I'm a veterinary technician here," the lady greeted us. "I'm going to ask you a few questions before you meet with the veterinarian."

"This is Sugar," I said, my voice sounding higher in pitch than normal. "And I'm Josie."

"And I'm Emily," added Mom. "Thank you for squeezing us in."

Our golden retriever leaned against my knee, and I could feel her heartbeat racing in her chest. "It's okay, girl. . . ." I bent down, whispering into her floppy ears. "Everything's going to be okay. I'm here." I brushed her soft back in long, gentle strokes, just in case her old ears didn't catch my words. I wanted Sugar to not only hear me, but feel me supporting her, too.

All my older siblings were working this morning, and Amelia went to a last-minute tap dancing class at the community center. Mom thought it was best if my little sister wasn't part of Sugar's appointments until we knew more, and I agreed with that, too. Amelia had a tough body, but her spirit was sensitive. Plus I didn't want her emotions making Sugar more nervous than she needed to be.

I inhaled through my nose and exhaled out my mouth, slowly, over and over, just like I used to when I was visualizing my gymnastics routines. I needed to be strong for Sugar right now. Mia asked us a bunch of questions—most of the same ones that Dr. Stern went through the other day—and reviewed her file, noting Sugar's chest X-ray and blood work had been emailed over.

"Now." Mia's expression softened, but she didn't smile. "Dr. Rodriguez will be in shortly."

"Thanks," Mom and I said in unison.

It felt like thirty minutes had passed before the door opened, and to my surprise it wasn't Dr. Rodriguez but Dad. "What'd I miss?" he said.

Mom yawned, triggering a yawn from me, too. "Nothing. We're still waiting for the vet."

Dad ruffled my hair. "How're you doing, kiddo? Hanging in there?"

I nodded. "Yeah, Dad. Thanks. Sugar seems nervous though."

Knock, knock.

"Hello?"

The door opened. An older man entered the room. "I'm Dr. Rodriguez, the neurologist," he said, greeting all of us. "And this must be Sugar."

"She's nervous," I blurted, and my cheeks grew hot. I guess I was a little nervous, too.

"Ahhhh." Dr. Rodriguez offered me a smile. He crouched down next to our dog, petting her head and letting her sniff his white coat. "Well, that's quite normal. This is a strange place, with lots of strange smells, isn't it, Sugar?" he said, and Sugar's tail began to wag. I felt my tensed-up shoulders relax and fall.

"What do you think's wrong with her, doctor?" asked Mom.

"Well, I've read through Sugar's file and spoken with Dr. Stern earlier today," began Dr. Rodriguez. "My recommendation is a full neuro exam. This would include a spinal tap and MRI. These tests will help rule out inflammation, infection, blood clots, and stroke. They can be completed today, here at our facility, upstairs. You could leave Sugar here for a few hours and pick her up this afternoon. An abdominal ultrasound may be helpful as well, but I think we should start with the full neuro and go from there, depending on what we find out."

The room fell silent. Dad pinched at the skin on his neck, something he did sometimes when he was thinking deeply. My parents exchanged a look. "This sounds . . .

very expensive," Dad said finally. "How much is all this going to cost?"

Dr. Rodriguez ran his palm down Sugar's back. "I understand your financial concerns. Our administrative team will certainly provide an estimate for you and talk about financing options. Can I answer any questions, in the meantime, about the particular tests?"

"So, you think something's wrong with Sugar's brain?" I asked him.

"I can't be certain right now, but based on Sugar's many symptoms, it does appear that something in the brain may be the root cause."

I felt my heart start to race. "Will you have to operate on her?"

Dr. Rodriguez looked into my eyes. "Let's not get ahead of ourselves," he said in a kind voice. "It's much too soon to determine if an operation would help Sugar. Okay?"

"Okay." I nodded. "Can I stay next to her during the tests?"

"Oh, I wish I could let you, but unfortunately owners aren't allowed to be in the room during procedures," said Dr. Rodriguez. "I promise Mia and I will take good care of her." He petted Sugar's head, and her tail wagged again. "She can even hang out with me in my office while I type up her appointment notes."

I bit my lip. Sugar *did* seem to like him. At Eastside Veterinary Clinic, there were lots of times that pet owners had to drop off their cats, dogs, birds, and all sorts of creatures with us. Sometimes the owners were okay with it, and other times they were uneasy. But I always knew inside that the animal was in great hands with Dr. Stern.

Watching Dr. Rodriguez with Sugar now, I felt a sense of peace come over me. Sugar would be okay with him, too. He was the neurologist, and he wanted to help her.

"Dad, Mom, we're doing all the tests, right?" I said, feeling tears sting at my eyes. "Sugar *needs* them. Dr. Rodriguez says so. It'll help us figure out how to fix her."

Mom reached for my hand, giving it a squeeze. "We'll talk with the front desk and figure out the details. Don't you worry about that for now."

Dad studied me for a moment. "Listen, kiddo." I met his eyes, feeling like I was fighting back tears. "You're doing an amazing job at the clinic, and I know you want to be there for Sugar. I'm super proud of you. But there is going to be a lot of waiting around today, and I have some things I want to talk to the doctor about, just us grown-ups. Why don't you and your mom go get ice cream, and then we'll meet up afterward?"

I wrapped my arms around Sugar's neck. "I'm not in the mood for ice cream, Dad, and I can't leave Sugar. She needs me." I attempted a smile. "But thanks anyway."

"Sweetie." Dad placed a gentle hand on my head. "This is a safe place. You heard Dr. Rodriguez—they'll be with her the entire time. You haven't been downtown in a while, so why don't you and your mom go do something fun, and I'll come meet up with you in a bit, okay? I promise I'll look after Sugar while I'm here."

Right then, Sugar licked my hand.

Mom smiled. "See? Sugar thinks that's a great idea, too. Josie, what do you say? Want to do something with your old mom while your dad wraps things up here? We never get to spend any one-on-one time together."

That was true. But it was also true that I didn't know Mom had noticed. I cracked my knuckles, a habit I'd picked up from watching Tom.

"Well . . . no offense, Dad . . ." I threw him a sly grin. "But you're like Sugar's least favorite human."

"Not today!" Dad opened up his palm to reveal a handful of light brown dog bones that I instantly recognized as Sugar's favorite treat. Our golden retriever caught a whiff of them and nuzzled her wet nose up against Dad's hand. "Only one now, Sugar! The rest are for later," Dad said, letting her snatch one dog bone before he tucked the other ones away in his pocket.

I had to laugh. Dad might not understand animals the way I did, but he understood one of the most important ways to get on Sugar's good side—through her belly! I bent down and wrapped my arms around her. I still didn't feel good about leaving Sugar at the specialist's office when she had these scary tests ahead of her, but Dr. Stern told me once that if you listen really closely, animals try to tell you how they feel, with energy and body language and sounds.

Sugar was wagging her tail, *thump thump*, against Dr. Rodriguez's leg. It wasn't tucked between her legs, either. It was a nice, perky tail. Her mouth flopped open, and her droopy tongue hung out. I listened to her breathing, and it sounded calm and even.

"You know, she does seem to be more relaxed," I said, giving her a final gentle squeeze. "Thanks, Dr. Rodriguez, for taking care of Sugar." Then I turned to my parents. "Okay, I'll go. But only if we get bubble tea, all right, Mom? I'm craving boba!"

Mom wrapped her arm around my shoulders. "I don't know what that is," she said, laughing, "but bubble tea it is!"

And she led me out the door.

Chapter 14

HEART TO HEART

I swung my feet beneath the park bench, staring out at the small city park stretched out in front of us. Mom and I sipped our bubble teas through thick straws until I finally broke the silence.

"Do you ever wish we lived in a big, fancy building like that one?" I asked her, pointing to a tall mostly windowed high-rise building down the block. "Miss Janice says her doorman carries in her groceries. And that there's always fresh-made coffee in the lobby."

Mom didn't laugh at my question. "That sounds lovely, but I don't wish for that, no," she said, sounding honest. "Why, do you?"

Slurp. "Not really. I like our townhouse." Then a sigh escaped my lips, even though I didn't mean for it to.

Normally Mom would press me with *What's wrong, Josie?* questions, but today, she didn't push it. She just let me talk at my own pace. "I do wish I had a cell phone sometimes, though. I'm like the only kid my age without one."

Mom's eyebrows pinched together. "Hmmm. Are you really? The *only* one, or are you exaggerating?"

I sighed. "Well, not the only one. . . . Sully doesn't have one. Yet, at least. But most of my friends have phones already."

"When you're fifteen like Sarah, we can talk about it."

I spun my straw around the ice. "That's like an eternity away, Mom."

I didn't bother telling her that I was missing out on tons of stuff that my friends were into. Maybe if I had my own SyncSong account, or if Lucy and I could text more often, things would be different with our friendship. Maybe we could hang out with Grace, and I would know what they were talking about when they used strange music-vocabulary words. Sometimes it felt like Lucy was the cool, grown-up one, and I was this babyish loser she was leaving behind.

"Do you eat these little black beads at the bottom?" Mom asked, pushing the big boba pearls around with her straw.

"*Yes,*" I said, feeling my face light up with a grin. "That's boba. It's soft, chewy balls of tapioca. It's the best part of bubble tea, Mom!" Mom didn't look convinced.

Mom slurped a black pearl up her straw and chewed on it thoughtfully.

I blinked, waiting. "Soooo? What do you think?"

"Not bad," she said, nodding after a moment. "But it's all a little too sweet for me."

"Mom!" I shook my head, laughing. "Bubble tea is life."

Mom laughed, too. "I think I'll stick with a coffee next time."

Slurp. It was nice hanging out with Mom alone. We rarely had these moments anymore. This seemed like the best time to talk to her about some of the things on my mind lately.

"Mom?"

"Yeah?"

I stopped swinging my legs and set my bubble tea down on the park bench. "Can we talk about something else?"

"Of course, Josie. Anything."

"Can you teach me how to put on makeup?"

Mom's gaze softened. "Hmmm. Well, makeup can be

a lot of fun, but you're only twelve, honey. I think you're a little too young to be wearing makeup on a regular basis, don't you?"

I felt my cheeks warm. So now I was too young for a cell phone and makeup? "I'm not talking about"—my mind flashed—"purple eye shadow or anything, although that'd be cool. More like concealer. To cover up . . . um . . . breakouts." Instinctively, I moved to touch the swollen spot on my chin.

"Oh." Mom's voice was higher in pitch, as if she was surprised. "I see. Sure, Josie. Of course I can help with that." She paused. "You know, honey, having pimples is a normal response to hormonal changes at your age. . . ."

"I *know*, Mom." I rolled my eyes. She didn't need to make this more embarrassing than it already was. My friends didn't really wear makeup, or at least, anything that I could notice. And Lucy had perfect skin—I bet she never had to wear concealer in her life!

I bit my lip, thinking. Maybe I should've waited until I was home alone and searched YouTube for tutorials. Maybe Mom just didn't understand what it was like to be an almost teenager these days. But Mom broke into my thoughts by gently elbowing me again.

"Josie, if it would make you feel more comfortable and confident, I'm happy to show you how to apply concealer. Just don't tell Amelia about your makeup tricks, or she'll get ideas and my favorite lipsticks will go missing. I can't have *all* my kids growing up this fast, you know."

I laughed, and it immediately released some tension in my body. Good. Mom was coming to terms with the fact I was actually growing up!

"Okay, okay, Mom. And since we're on the subject, I . . . I need deodorant. Like to wear every day, not just the old workout one in my gymnastics bag. That tube is half melted anyway."

"Sure, sweetie. We can pick everything up from the drugstore today. And . . . thank you for opening up to me, Josie. It's not always easy to know when girls your age are ready for certain things."

For some reason, her comment made me burst out laughing. "We're not that complicated, Mom. Just concealer, deodorant, a cell phone, and bubble tea. See? Easy!"

"Not easy." Mom met my eyes, smiling. "Pigs and puppies, too, remember?"

"Well, since you brought it up, maybe *one itty-bitty adorable and well-behaved* puppy?"

Mom pulled her sunglasses down over her eyes. "Nice try." Her phone buzzed, and she quickly reached for it, reading a text message. I felt my heart rate skyrocket.

"Is it Dad?"

"Yes. He's ready for us to head back now. They're done with Sugar's tests, and Dr. Rodriguez will go over the results with us together."

"Let's go!" I hopped off the bench and tossed my empty bubble tea cup into the nearby recycling bin. Another text message beeped on Mom's phone, and she paused, reading it. Her eyebrows pinched together. "What is it?" I asked her.

"You know, why don't we just meet Dad back at home?" Mom suggested. "Dad can chat with Dr. Rodriguez now while we grab the bus."

"But I want to see Sugar." I shook my head. "And I want to hear what the doctor has to say."

"Well, it sounds like Dr. Rodriguez is ready for the consultation now, and I'm not sure he can wait another twenty minutes for us to get there. He's a very busy neurologist, Josie, and his whole team did us a big favor by squeezing in Sugar today. Dad will listen to everything he needs to say, and he'll share the news with us tonight, okay?"

I sighed. I understood how busy veterinarians could get, but still, I was disappointed. I wanted to be there for Sugar, and going home without her beside me felt like a betrayal of trust. "But they'll both come right home afterward? And Dad will give us the full recap?"

Mom smiled, and I felt her reassurance wash over me. I trusted my parents, and I knew they loved Sugar as much as us kids did. "Full recap," she said. "Dad and Sugar. Promise."

"Okay." I stretched my arms above my head, squinting through the sunlight into the grassy park ahead. I looked at Mom, and in the reflection of her sunglasses, I saw a sly grin creep across my face. "Are we heading to that bus stop over there?"

"Yes."

"Race you to the street!"

I bolted across the park before my mom could protest. She wasn't much of a runner, but her labored laughter floated into my ears as she sprinted behind me.

Once we both reached the bus stop, giggling and

trying to catch our breath, Mom said, "Wasn't a fair race! You didn't count to three."

"You sound like Amelia!" I said, and Mom grinned, loading more money into our bus passes in a little machine on the sidewalk.

Dad was right—I didn't often come this far into the city, so it was a fun bus ride home. It wasn't too crowded, so I scored a window seat and stared at the city as we whizzed through it, admiring the mix of new, modern buildings alongside older architecture. It was a beautiful, sunny summer day, and it seemed like everyone downtown was out and about, even though it was a regular weekday. We hopped off a stop before our usual one in front of the library, near the perimeter of the city limits, where a small pharmacy was located. Mom and I zipped through our shopping, and she helped me pick out things she thought I'd like.

As we walked home with the pharmacy bag swinging in my hand, I imagined what Grace must've felt moving from glamorous California to our little neighborhood tucked away in Columbus. Dad's old boss used to make fun of our neighborhood. Dad told me once that some people thought our neighborhood should be bought up by developers and turned into high-rises, or renovated to be fancy lofts.

Maybe we didn't have fancy amenities, but I had meant what I told Mom—I liked our townhouse just fine. It was our home. I loved that my friends' stoops were all right next to each other, and how every time you went outside, you saw someone you knew. Especially now that I had my own concealer and deodorant!

When we got to our stoop, I looked around for the van, but it wasn't there. "Maybe you should text Dad and tell him to drop Sugar off in front, before he parks too far away for her to walk," I suggested.

Mom gently tugged on my ponytail. "He'll call if he needs us. Now, let's see. Where's my key?"

She unlocked the door and turned the doorknob. As I walked into the foyer and kicked off my shoes, howling echoed off the walls from somewhere inside the house. From where I stood, I could see the living room curtains had been torn down, and there were scratch marks in the exposed white paint.

"What in the world?" I said.

"MILLIE? Are you home?" Mom called out in alarm. "Sarah? Ellen? Tom?"

Muddy paw prints looked like stamps across the wooden floors, and Mom and I exchanged a look.

"The puppies!" we said at the same time, and rushed into the living room.

Chapter 15

SICK AS A DOG

The curtains were crumpled on the floor, and they were barking. Well, the curtains weren't barking *exactly*—it was what was underneath them. The wrinkled fabric now completely covered the big dog crate in the corner of the living room, and the puppies yipped and whined.

I tugged at the white-and-gray patterned curtains, feeling a rush of relief flood over me as I saw the puppies happily pawing over each other, clambering to reach me. They were lucky they'd been inside the protective metal bars of the crate, or the heavy curtains could've crushed them.

"What do you think happened?" I asked Mom as I unlocked the crate and gave each puppy a once-over.

Mom's gaze shifted to the ceiling. "Those curtains

have been up for years . . . ," she mumbled, piecing the mystery together. "I don't think they'd just fall down. . . ." Her eyes went to the paw prints in the hall.

"I'd better make sure everyone's accounted for. . . . One . . . two . . . three . . ." I snuggled each puppy close as I counted them all. "Four . . . five . . ." I didn't even need to finish counting them all. I knew exactly who was missing. "Speedy!" I said to Mom, feeling anger seep into my voice. "Amelia probably took Speedy out. That one's her favorite. When did her tap dancing class end?"

Mom glanced at the clock on her cell phone. "An hour ago. But Sarah was going to take her to the library afterward. I'll check upstairs, but you need to take those puppies out before they have an accident in the house."

I nodded. Mom had a point. Their padded mat on the bottom of the crate didn't have any messes, so they probably needed to go soon. I'd read that puppies needed a consistent schedule to help with housebreaking. They clawed all over me, yelping and biting each other playfully. After a nap, these pups sure had energy to burn, and I definitely didn't want to clean up seven accidents on our rug.

I quickly hooked leashes to collars and led the bounding fur balls out the back door to our little patio area.

"Greetings!" boomed a loud voice, and I practically jumped out of my skin.

"Tom! Why are you always popping up like that?! Just tell people when you're around. Geez!"

"That's why I said *greetings*. By way of greeting. Obviously."

My brother was wearing his bathing suit, stretched out on a plastic lawn chair with a tattered beach towel flopped across the back of it. Tom was so pale, his skin practically glowed in the bright sunlight, and I was pretty sure he was wearing one of Mom's cheap pairs of sunglasses. He looked ridiculous!

I bit back a smirk. It was one of those moments I wished I had a cell phone. I would've loved to take a picture of him as payback for making fun of my body odor the other day!

The puppies tugged me down the steps to our little grassy area. As they sniffed around and did their business, I asked Tom, "Where's Amelia?"

"Haven't seen her," he said, his voice sounding half-asleep.

"Well, what about the living room curtains?" I demanded. "Have you seen them? Because they're *on the floor*."

"Haven't seen them either."

The cordless house phone rang, and Tom answered it. "Greetings! Shilling house!"

I rolled my eyes. Couldn't he say *hello* like a normal person? I swear, he was like a giant ten-year-old sometimes. Then he extended the phone out into the air.

"It's for youuuu," he singsonged.

I reached for the phone, careful not to step on Blue, who had been winding her leash around my leg. "Hello?" Then I scolded, "Blue, quit tripping me!"

"Josie?"

"Oh!" I stood upright in surprise at the voice on the other end of the line. "Hey, Sully."

Tom tore off his sunglasses dramatically, as if he was suspicious at the change in my tone. He threw me a knowing smile. I felt my cheeks redden. *Great.* I didn't need my brother, the biggest teaser in the whole city, to know I had a crush on my next-door neighbor!

Sully hardly *ever* called me. I cleared my throat and tried to sound casual. "What's up?"

"Did Fernanda find you?"

"No?"

"Oh. She's really bummed you didn't come swimming at the Y with us today."

I face-palmed. "Ohhhhh, I forgot. I'm so sorry! But I was at the vet all morning—not Eastside, this emergency hospital—and then there was a bubble tea thing with my mom. Ugh. Is Fernanda super mad?"

"Well, kinda," Sully admitted. "We got back a little bit ago. Carlos called a meeting, but we need you there. I think they're on my front steps now. Just wanted to make sure you knew. I mean, in case you didn't see the bike chain or something."

Houdini climbed on top of Amelia's fallen bike, and I lifted him up, setting him back down on the grass. If any of the puppies were going to puzzle his or her way out of the backyard, it would be Houdini.

"Things are a little—*er*"—I looked around at the puppies, sniffing and peeing and exploring—"busy right now. Is the meeting an emergency?"

"Dunno. But Carlos said to bring the puppies."

"Oh! Well, that's a good sign, right?" I grinned. "I've got them on their leashes now!"

"Okay, cool. See you in five."

"See you in five!"

I clicked off the phone and tossed it back to Tom, who caught it like the first-string football star he was. I waited for him to say something about a boy calling me, but instead, he squirted sunblock onto his hand and lathered up his face and neck.

"Tell Mom I'm next door, okay?" I asked him, leading the puppies to the back gate.

"If she comes out here, I will." Tom placed his hands behind his head, relaxing backward. "But this hardworking barista is off. The. Clock." He emphasized each word dramatically.

"Whatever. She'll come looking for me eventually. Just don't forget to tell her when you see her, okay?"

"Yeah, yeah. Don't worry. I'm not ready for Mom to go all SOS during my crucial light therapy time. I'm making Vitamin K right now. Wait. Or is it D?"

Right then, we overhead Mom in the house, giving Amelia a stern talking-to. I looked over through the back-door window, and I could see my sister looking guilty and cradling Speedy in her arms.

"Mom! I'm going next door!" I yelled.

Tom grunted. "You're blocking my light."

"Whatever. Just tell Mom I'm with my friends if she comes out here! C'mon, pups," I said, tugging them along.

I unhinged the back gate of our tall, wooden fence. It led to a little alley that we shared with Sully's family next door, where we all kept our garbage cans and recycling bins. The puppies happily padded right at my heels as we slipped through the back gate and into the alley, and nearly bumped right into Dad's back.

"Dad?" I said, fear seizing my body as I took in my surroundings. "What's wrong?" Dad was bent down, hunched over Sugar, who was lying on the alley cement and shaking. Dad's eyes were moist. He seemed just as surprised to see me as I was to see what was happening. "Dad?" I repeated, dropping down beside him. I placed a hand on Sugar's fur, feeling her body seize. "Is this a reaction from her tests today?" I whispered, afraid to speak too loudly.

"No, honey." He shook his head. "The antiseizure medication isn't working."

"Should we call Dr. Rodriguez? Dr. Stern? What do we do?!"

"It'll pass in a moment, Josie." He squeezed my hand and said calmly, "Don't be afraid."

Dad was right. Sugar's body stopped shaking about a minute later, and she slowly opened her eyes, just like the last time she had a seizure. It was strange, the way it looked as if she was just waking up from a nap, when I knew something terrible was going on deep inside her body.

"Oh, Sugar, I'm so sorry you're sick," I said, feeling tears sting at my eyes. The puppies seemed to agree with me. Lucky nuzzled right up into her long golden fur, and Houdini went straight for her mouth, pressing his little nose against her twitching whiskers.

I studied Dad, and I could almost hear the gears in his brain shifting, grinding together, and working through a problem.

"Do you think Sugar can walk?" I asked. "Or should we carry her? Tom's out back—"

Dad took the puppy leashes from my hands. "Get Tom," he said, his expression solemn.

He didn't have to ask me twice.

Chapter 16

RUFF RESULTS

I stared at the mantel above the fireplace, where Mom had placed the framed article about Hamlet from the *City Centennial*, and waited for my parents to share the news with all of us kids.

"Sugar has a brain tumor," Dad explained. "The tests today confirmed it. Dr. Rodriguez—he's the neurologist—said it's a large one, and it's compressing."

I felt my stomach lurch, like I was going to fall, and I reached for the couch arm to steady myself. Sugar had a *tumor*? In her *brain*? This couldn't be happening!

I blinked. Mom's lips moved. Dad nodded. Ellen leaned forward, cradling her chin in her palms. It felt like I was sitting in the middle of a movie with a broken film reel. I was only getting bits and pieces of information, but they didn't fit together, because there was no way our dog could have a brain tumor.

I scratched the top of Lucky's head, trying to slow my racing heartbeat. The puppy licked my cheek, and my eyes glazed over with tears.

"What does that mean?" Amelia asked my parents.

"It means that Sugar's condition is not treatable," said Mom, placing a hand on Amelia's shoulder. "I'm so sorry, honey."

"Why can't the doctor remove the tumor?" Sarah asked. I noticed her hands were shaking, and I looked down at my own to see that they were shaking, too.

"I wish he could, but I'm sorry, kids." Dad's voice broke, and he covered his face with his hands. Tom reached over and patted his back—*once, twice*—like I'd seen Dad do to him so many times before after football games. Dad's chest heaved, and finally he dropped his hands, and Amelia gasped, seeing the tears on my Dad's face.

"She just needs more tests," said Ellen, trying to reason everything away. "Yes, Sugar's old, but there's got to be something else that can fix her besides surgery. Radiation?"

"We did all the tests Dr. Rodriguez recommended,"

Mom said. "And we were lucky the specialist's office was able to give us financial aid, which helped cover the costs of the MRI and spinal tap. Otherwise I don't think we would've been able to afford them. . . ."

Sarah sighed deeply. "So . . . are you saying that Sugar's *dying*?"

My parents exchanged a look, and they both nodded. "I'm so, so, sorry," said Dad, his voice choking again. Amelia burst into tears.

"We have to do SOMETHING!" she wailed. "We can't just let her die! She's the best dog in the world!"

I didn't agree with Amelia on many things these days, but she was absolutely right about that—Sugar *was* the best dog in the world. She'd been part of our family since I was only a few months old. I didn't know how to live without her.

She was always there when I came home from school, or hanging with the Three Stoops crew, like a loyal friend. She always listened when I needed someone to talk to, when I knew the people around me wouldn't understand. She accepted first the pig, and now the puppies, into our family without any complaints.

My jaw went numb, as if I was going to throw up. I cradled my stomach, leaning forward. Sugar had always been there for me. I'd been so busy with gymnastics, and then Hamlet, and the veterinary clinic, and now the litter, that I hadn't focused on her much this year.

I lay down on the rug next to Sugar's big, soft body. Soon the puppies all made their way toward us, too, curling up against my back, and tugging at my shoelaces, and whining against my hands, angling for a back scratch.

Mom reached over and squeezed Sarah's hand. "Sugar's quality of life is going to decline, possibly very rapidly," Mom said.

My chest tightened as I stroked Sugar's fur, trying not to imagine the tumor in there, pressing down on her brain, stealing her away from us.

"How rapidly?" Ellen asked.

"It's hard to know for sure. . . ." Dad frowned. "But I think we should all be prepared for the worst. I know this is hard for all of us. Sugar is a part of our family." The living room filled with the soft, muffled sound of crying.

Sugar was dying.

I pressed my face against our dog and squeezed my eyes shut, feeling tears slide down the bridge of my nose. Sugar's golden fur turned wet against my face, and I wondered if she could feel how much I loved her inside my heart.

"Is she in pain right now?" asked Ellen softly. I opened my eyes and watched as my older sister reached over and gently placed a hand on Sugar's back.

"I don't know, sweetheart," Dad said. "I think she probably is. Dr. Rodriguez gave us some medicine to help her feel better. And we'll monitor the progression of her symptoms closely before we decide what to do."

Amelia sobbed even harder. "But if there's no cure, we can't DO anything!"

My parents exchanged another look, and my mom glanced at Sarah. "We need to seriously consider putting Sugar to sleep." *Putting Sugar to sleep.* I had heard Dr. Stern and Daniel talk about this at the clinic, so I knew what it meant even if Millie didn't. There was an injection that the vet could give a pet, when it was very sick, old, or in severe pain, that would make them go to sleep and not wake up. "It will help her to pass away peacefully," Mom said. Tom put his arm around me, and I leaned against him. "I know this is so hard for you all. . . . It's hard for us, too. We love Sugar so much," Mom said. "But we need to think about her quality of life, and what's the most compassionate next step."

There was a knock at the front door. No one in the living room moved. Finally, I heard Tom shift from the couch and the swing of the door on its hinges.

"Is Josie around?" said a perky voice.

Lucy.

I squeezed my eyes shut again. When they were closed, and I just felt the little thumps of puppy heartbeats and the soft fur of Sugar against my skin, I could forget that my beloved dog was dying, these seven puppies were homeless, Mrs. Taglioni was moving away, Grace hated me, and I didn't know if Lucy and I were really best friends anymore.

"Josie?"

I opened my eyes, and Lucy stood next to my brother in the living room doorway. She shifted her balance from one leg to the other, a move I'd seen her do a million times before vault, the apparatus that made her the most nervous. I sighed. Great. I missed swimming at the Y *and* the Three Stoops meeting. I bet my friends wouldn't let me hear the end of it.

"Hi, everyone." Lucy gave a half-hearted wave. I didn't bother smiling. She could tell from the energy in the room that something serious was going on, so there was no need to fake it. "Josie, I was . . . um . . . well, we're all outside."

My throat tightened. I didn't trust myself to speak without crying, so I just stared at her, blinking.

"Hi, Lucy. We're wrapping up a family meeting," Mom said. She smiled, but her eyes caught the light, and I could still see the sadness radiating from her face. "Josie can go outside in a few minutes, if she likes."

I cleared my throat. "Be right out, Luce."

"Okay. See you," she said, seeing herself out the front door.

I studied my parents. "So . . . what do we do now?"

"We wait and watch Sugar's symptoms progress," Dad said. "And then we'll take it from there."

I nodded. "And I think we need to talk to Dr. Stern for a second opinion."

Ellen said softly, "Josie, this doesn't sound like a situation that requires a second opinion. . . ."

"I would just feel better about it if I heard Dr. Stern's opinion, okay!"

"Okay, Josie." Mom nodded. "I think I'd feel better with Cassandra's opinion, too."

"Good." My throat clenched up, but I got out the words I'd been thinking about. "I want to take Sugar to the farm to see Hamlet, Sugar hasn't seen her since she moved away. And she'd get to smell all kinds of new things, like the field of daffodils, and horses, and hay. Maybe it would cheer her up a bit, you know? Could we call Mr. Upton and Mrs. Taglioni? Maybe drive out there on Saturday?"

I couldn't bear the thought that Sugar might not make it a few more days. Mom looked at Dad and then nodded. "I think that would be okay," she said. "How about we all go? A family trip?"

"Yes!" said my little sister, practically leaping to her feet.

"Definitely," Tom said. "I'll try to change my shift schedule so I'm not working. Though it'll be hard to replace a barista of this caliber." He rubbed his scruffy chin.

Even though Tom liked to lift our moods with his sense of humor, it wasn't working for me today. I still felt horrible inside.

"That's enough talk for tonight, everyone. Josie, why don't you meet up with your friends?" Mom suggested. "Millie and I will feed the dogs and take them out back."

Amelia wiped her eyes. "Really, Mom? Josie . . . is that okay? Can I help?"

I lifted Speedy into Amelia's lap and said, "Of course it's okay. You're a really good helper, Millie. And maybe tomorrow you can help me puppy proof." I motioned to the curtains on the floor beneath the living room window. "Any idea how that all happened?"

Amelia's cheeks turned a soft shade of pink. She glanced at my parents, but they both smiled at her, and we could tell they weren't mad. "Um . . . *maybe* it was a tug-of-war between Blue and Tugger . . . ," Amelia said. "Tugger won."

Mom called Amelia to the kitchen to help her, and Sugar's collar jingled as she got to her feet, catching the scent of food with her nose. At least she still had some appetite—for now, anyway.

I gave our dog a quick hug, whispered *love you* in her ear, and slipped out the front door. My friends waited on Sully's stoop, whispering. They looked up and stopped talking as soon as they heard my door open.

"If you guys are talking about me, why do you even want me here right now?" I snapped, not meaning to sound as harsh as I did.

"Where were you today?" asked Fernanda, her voice sounding hurt. "I tried knocking before we left, and no one answered."

"I'm sorry, it's just—I had to go to the vet, and—" I noticed Lucy roll her eyes and a surge of fury exploded inside me. I was dealing with a lot right now, and I really needed a friend. Why did she have to change so much this summer? "*Why* are you being so mean to me?" I said, my voice rising.

"Me, being mean to you?" Lucy scoffed. "Whatever."

"No, NOT whatever!"

Lucy stomped down Sully's steps and started walking home. "Where're you going?" I called out after her. "I thought there was a meeting . . . ?"

"Have the meeting WITHOUT ME!" she yelled back over her shoulder. "I don't even CARE! I can solve the Case of the New Neighbor on my own!"

"Fine! Why don't you text Grace and have a new best friend then, too!"

Lucy spun around, her eyes practically sparking with fury. "MAYBE I WILL!"

"FINE!" Blood pumped fast in my veins. I turned toward Fernanda, blinking back tears. "Listen, I'm really sorry about missing the pool today. And Carlos, Sully, you guys, too. It's been . . . today's been the WORST. I didn't mean to leave you guys hanging. The pool would've been fun. And I could really use some fun right now."

Fernanda's expression softened. "It's okay, Josie," she said gently. "Next time."

"Yeah," Carlos echoed.

Sully palmed his basketball, exchanging it between his hands, and said nothing. It all felt like too much. Losing Lucy, Mrs. Taglioni, and now Sugar, too. I was too exhausted to hold back the tears any longer. I broke down crying, turned around, stomped up my stoop steps, and let the door slam behind me, ignoring my friends as they called after me.

Chapter 17

KEEP CALM AND CARRY ON

I had hoped Dr. Rodriguez was wrong about Sugar's diagnosis. But things got way worse, and fast. Sugar had another seizure and stopped eating altogether. On Friday morning, Amelia found her in the corner of the living room, just circling and circling, as if she was caught in a tail chase she couldn't stop.

Mom tried to pull Sugar out of her trancelike state, calming the dog down until she fell asleep on the floor. Then Mom retreated to her bedroom, and I'm pretty sure she called Dad to tell him what happened. Amelia was upset, too, so I asked her to help me fill up the dogs' water bowls in the kitchen so she'd have something productive to do.

All I wanted was to distract myself from my worries,

so I stuck to my normal Friday-morning schedule at Eastside.

I stood in an examination room, watching Daniel wrap his arms around an oversized cat crate.

"Catch," he said, "or dump?"

I studied the anxious cat meowing inside the crate. "Um . . . dump, I guess?"

Usually I wasn't allowed to touch the animals that came into Eastside for checkups, but today was different. Mrs. Taglioni's cat, Tootsie, was on the table, and my neighbor wanted me to get as much hands-on experience at the veterinary clinic as I was allowed, which sounded good to me. It turned out *catch-and-dump* was the phrase that Daniel and Dr. Stern used for humanely coaxing an anxious cat out of a crate. If it was done right, the people looking over the cat wouldn't get scratched or bitten in the process.

But if done *wrong* . . .

"Your parents signed a waiver, right?" Daniel pressed his brows together.

"Um . . . I think so?"

"I gave her a tranquilizer, so she should be on good behavior," chimed in Mrs. Taglioni, patting her twisted, dark bun of hair. She didn't sound worried at all, but then she added, "Well, she is meowing. I suppose you never know with cats. . . ."

My heart beat a little faster. Animals weren't always their best selves at the vet's office—I'd seen this first-hand too many times lately. They were scared or hungry or feeling sick or even confused, and those emotions always fired off a bunch of defensive instincts, like fight-or-flight.

Plus, this was *Tootsie*. She was practically legendary for being feisty. Sugar had gotten many scratches over the years to prove it.

Also, Tootsie attacked Hamlet one time, many months ago, when our pig busted the back fence and bolted into Mrs. Taglioni's townhouse. I was betting that Tootsie was more the fighting kind of cat than the fleeing kind. If Daniel was the catcher, he could handle that situation from the front lines!

"Definitely dump," I said.

"Okay. Gentle now," said Daniel as we positioned ourselves. "Here we go. . . . It's okay, Tootsie. . . . Nice and slow now, Josie. . . ."

I wrapped my arms around the plastic crate, pulse racing, as Daniel wiggled his fingers in front of the metal door and counted softly, *"One . . . two . . . three!"*

I lifted up the back of the crate with both arms just as Daniel opened up the wire door. Tootsie gently slid out and onto the cool metal of the examination table and into Daniel's open arms. Daniel stroked her head and let her sniff his hands. I exhaled in relief. I'd done my first successful feline catch-and-dump!

Tootsie's hair stood on end as she absorbed the unfamiliar surroundings, but Daniel cooed softly, "Everything's fine. . . . Good Tootsie, gooooood Tootsie. . . ."

"What's wrong with her, Mrs. Taglioni?" I asked. "Why is she here?"

"Oh, nothing at all. I just want to make sure she's right as rain before we move to the farm. You can imagine, Tootsie does not like seeing all our belongings getting boxed up, no, not at all. She's constantly pacing and meowing and pawing at my socks when I'm trying to sleep."

There was a gentle knock at the door, and Dr. Stern popped her head inside. "Hello, Molly. Hello, Tootsie, it's good to see you!"

Dr. Stern's pleasant demeanor was like sunshine. She and Daniel took Tootsie's temperature, listened to her heartbeat, and checked her eyes, ears, and paws.

"Everything looks good," Dr. Stern said finally at the

end of the exam. "Are you getting excited about the big move, Molly?"

Mrs. Taglioni glanced my way, and I wondered if she was worried about hurting my feelings. So I said, "Go ahead, Mrs. Taglioni—we all saw the sign in your window. If I was moving in with Hamlet, I'd be pretty excited, too! I really want to hear the details."

My longtime neighbor laughed. "Well, it will be a relief in some ways, especially to help out my brother, Mike. His kids sure are helpful, and they'll be around quite a lot, too, so it'll be nice to have company visiting all the time. I'll miss the townhouse and the neighborhood and all of *you*, of course, but I do hope you'll come visit, and often."

"I'll be there at least once a month," I promised. "By the way, did Mom call you? About us visiting tomorrow, and bringing Sugar and the puppies, too?" My palms began to sweat as I felt all eyes on me at the mention of our golden retriever.

Mrs. Taglioni nodded. I wondered if Mom had told her the news. "She did, and Mike said that's just fine. I won't be able to make it, unfortunately—just some moving things to deal with—but my brother said he's looking forward to your visit."

Hooray!

"Do you need help packing anything up? We can help you."

"No, my dear. I hired some strong movers to deal with all of that. But thank you." Mrs. Taglioni winked. "Now, Dr. Stern, I could use tips with helping Tootsie adjust to life on the farm. What do I do if she wants to become a full-time outdoor cat? I'm a little concerned she'll move into the barn, and there's this adorable chipmunk that I'd like to have stick around for a while. . . ."

Dr. Stern shared strategies for protecting Chip the chipmunk from the prowling house cat. Then, we secured Tootsie back in her crate, and Daniel recorded the appointment in the cat's chart. Finally, after Mrs. Taglioni's questions were all answered, Dr. Stern and I had a minute alone in her office.

My gaze flicked to her diplomas on the wall, and I remembered last Christmas, sitting in this very space and her telling me about how to ask animals how they feel, and listening to the different ways they could communicate.

"You're awfully quiet today. Do you want to talk about something?" Dr. Stern said, lifting a ballpoint pen from a prescription pad.

I shrugged. "Yes . . . and no."

She nodded, leaning forward onto her desk. "Dr. Rodriguez sent over Sugar's test results." I picked at my fingernails, listening. "I'm sorry about the diagnosis," she continued. "I know it must've been difficult news to hear. And a hard thing to deal with." Dr. Stern backed off, listening, and something about the way she gave a room space and a person time to breathe always set me at ease.

"The antiseizure medication isn't working," I said, feeling my eyes well up. "Mom and Dad said she'll get worse . . . that they're trying to help her be as comfortable as possible until, you know, the end." Dr. Stern sat back in her chair, patiently waiting until I was ready to share more. "They mentioned that Sugar might need to be put to sleep. Do you think she's scared . . . or in pain?"

Dr. Stern watched me, a solemn expression on her face. "It's possible that she's in pain, yes. Sugar's brain tumor is quite advanced."

I blinked back tears. I hated asking this question, but I needed to know. I trusted Dr. Stern like I trusted my parents. She didn't treat me like a baby and sugarcoat things—I knew she'd give it to me straight, and straight truth was what I needed to hear right now.

"Do you think we should? Put her to sleep?"

"Oh, Josie. That's not for me to say. It's a family decision, and I know it's a really, really hard one."

I couldn't hold back the tears anymore. "But I don't want her to die."

"Oh, I know, Josie, I know. But remember that Sugar has lived a long, wonderful life as your dog. She loves you all so much. You gave her a wonderful home." Dr. Stern handed me a tissue, and I took it, pressing it to my dripping nose.

"Do you think it's okay to bring Sugar out to the farm, to see Hamlet, one last time? We were going to go tomorrow."

"I think Sugar will probably enjoy a little adventure. Remember, you're her pack, and she's happiest when she's with you all. You could bring her favorite treats, too, perhaps? She might be more sleepy than normal, but a nice, shady, and relaxing day outside is always good for a dog. Just keep an eye on her, offer fresh water at all times, and allow her plenty of rest."

I nodded. "Would it be okay if I helped out here for a bit longer today?"

The veterinarian smiled and reached her hand across

her desk, placing it on top of mine and giving me a squeeze.

"You're welcome to stay as long as you'd like, as long as it's okay with your parents," she said. "And I'm here if you'd like to talk about anything more."

"Thanks, Dr. Stern."

Daniel popped his head into the office and said, "Josie? Your sister's here with the puppies."

"Sister?" I raised an eyebrow. "Amelia walked here by herself?"

"No, um." Daniel raised his eyes to the ceiling. He'd met Amelia a bunch of times when she came to the clinic to visit Dr. Stern's son, Lou. "A different sister . . . an older one? You've never mentioned her before. And your friend . . . Sully?"

Sully was here?

I felt heat creep up my throat.

"Thank you, Daniel. Now's actually a great time to take a look at how the puppies are doing," said Dr. Stern. "Josie?"

I followed her into the main lobby area. Miss Janice was kneeling down, petting the puppies and chatting with Ellen and Sully.

"Look how much they've grown in just a few days!" Miss Janice gushed.

"Ellen? Sully? What're you guys doing here?" I said. "I thought Mom was bringing the puppies over. . . ."

Ellen smiled. "I had nothing to do today. Just thought I'd help out."

I glanced at Sully, and he spun his baseball cap and said, "Yeah, I was sitting on the stoop and bored, is all." He shrugged again. "Figured I'd check out this whole vet thing, you know?"

"Oh! Okay. Cool." I swear my heart skipped a beat. Because I didn't want him bringing up the last time we saw each other, when I started bawling my eyes out and abandoned the Three Stoops meeting, I quickly added, "So, Miss Janice . . . have you heard about anyone wanting to adopt a puppy?"

Her eyes sparkled. "You know, now that you mention it, Malek Johnson talked about getting another dog the other day. . . ."

"Oh, that's great!" Sully said, snapping his fingers. "I love shooting hoops with Mr. Johnson. He's the coolest."

I grinned. Mr. Johnson was a super-friendly man, probably in his late thirties, who lived a few streets over with his girlfriend. He already had a friendly dog named Gruff. As long as Gruff liked other dogs, Mr. Johnson was the perfect candidate to adopt a puppy!

"Houdini might be a good option for Mr. Johnson," I suggested. "Do you think you could call him, Miss Janice? Houdini's super sweet and a bundle of energy. But our friends get first pick, so I would just need to double-check with them. . . ."

"I don't think you need to," said Sully with a sly grin. He reached over and picked up Babbles. "They've claimed this one."

I matched his knowing look. "Ha! We'll see, Sull. It's got to be a unanimous vote."

"You tell Fernanda that."

"Well, she *is* a powerful beauty, isn't she?" Miss Janice scratched Babbles's head. "I'll give Mr. Johnson a call this afternoon, Josie. That might work out nicely."

"And guess what," I said, remembering. "A few emails came through last night in response to our Dog Days Adoptathon next week! We're going to host it in front of the Three Stoops. Do you think you all can make it?"

"That sounds wonderful," said Dr. Stern. "I'm sure you'll have lots of interest in these cute animals, Josie. Please go ahead and take them to exam room three. I'll meet you in there in a minute."

Dr. Stern reached for the puppies' files and retreated back to her office. I set Lucky down on the floor tiles, and Ellen passed me the handful of leashes. "I'll wait here," my sister said as Daniel lingered back and asked casually, "Soooooo . . . do you go to college around here?"

When Sully and I disappeared down the hallway, I whispered, "I've never seen Daniel so friendly before."

Sully laughed. "Or Ellen. It's weird."

"Yeah," I said as the puppies bounded at our heels. "Totally weird!"

Before we turned into exam room 3, Sully spun to face me and stopped in his tracks, making his sneakers squeak on the floor tiles. We stared at each other in the hallway. My heart skipped a beat. The bright corridor lights illuminated his face.

He looked at me for a second, like he wanted to say something, but his eyebrows were twitching in this weird way.

Then he finally said, "Um, so there was something I wanted to—" but his voice cracked and he stopped talking. His cheeks flamed with patches of red. He tugged the brim of his hat down, covering his face in embarrassment.

Being around Sully made my insides flutter, and I couldn't help a smile from spreading across my face. "Uh . . . you okay, Sully?"

He lifted the hat back up but kept his gaze locked on his shoes. "So remember how we—" he started, but then Dr. Stern interrupted from behind us.

"You ready?"

I spun around. My face burned with heat. "Um, yep! Exam room three!"

I imagined what I'd text Lucy about this, if we were talking. *Sully's acting like he has a secret or something!*

I picked up Houdini and snuggled him close. Because if there's anything that can help erase weirdness around boys, it's a puppy.

Chapter 18

DEATH'S DOOR

If I ever thought Sully visiting me at Eastside was the most exciting thing that could happen to me on a shift, I soon discovered I was wrong. After Ellen and Sully had taken the puppies back home, while Miss Janice was on lunch break and Dr. Stern and Daniel were in surgery, a girl barreled through the front door of the clinic, completely breathless.

I looked up from feeding the Kingdom, startled.

"You work here?" the girl asked. Well. She wasn't really a *girl*. She could've been my brother's age, nineteen or twenty, maybe home on college break just like him. I searched her face, wondering if she knew Tom or Ellen or maybe even Sarah, but nothing about her looked familiar.

"Uh, sort of? Not really *work*," I said, because I didn't, not officially. I was too young for a real job. There were also laws about that sort of thing, at least according to Dad. I was more of a helper. It was like my version of pet sitting and going to summer school and shadowing a professional, all at the same time. "And—um—we're closed right now."

"But it's an emergency! I hit a turtle," the girl said, extending her arms. It looked like the turtle was wrapped up in an old brown blanket, and I couldn't see how badly the reptile was hurt. "Well, *I* didn't hit it," she quickly clarified. "The car in front of me hit it. Then they just drove off! I barely slammed on the brakes in time. I thought it was a goner, but then it looked like it was squirming or moving or something? I don't know, I mean, it's a *turtle* so it wasn't like making a lot of noise, you know? But maybe it's still alive? I only had this blanket in the car, and I didn't want it to bite me. Ughhhh, this just sucks. I'm running so late and I'm double-parked out front—"

"Shh!" I said, narrowing my eyes at her. "Lower your voice." If there was anything I knew about injured animals, it was that loud noises could frighten them. Animals that were afraid were more likely to react in negative ways, like biting, trembling, running away, or in the case of a shy, quiet turtle—*dying*.

We weren't an emergency animal hospital. There was one of those downtown. We were just a tiny neighborhood clinic that treated dogs, cats, and pocket pets, like guinea pigs and mice.

I stared at the blanket. Drops of blood splattered the side of the fabric. Things didn't look promising for the poor turtle already. I felt myself start to hyperventilate.

Breathe. Breathe.

My mind raced. Was she going to unwrap the turtle right there, in the middle of the clinic lobby, while the veterinary staff were tied up in surgery and I was completely untrained to treat the turtle's injuries?! I suddenly felt my cheeks tingle like I was going to throw up, but I tried to push the sensation out of my mind.

"Set the turtle down here," I told the girl. I brushed loose sheets of paperwork off the front desk to clear a space. I'd organize them again before Miss Janice got back. "Careful now!" I gently pulled back the blanket to get a closer look at the turtle and gasped. There were two big cracks in its shell, and the pieces were starting to separate.

"You can fix it, right?" said the girl, her eyes wide.

"Let me think for a second." I sounded calmer and wiser than I felt inside, but everything I'd observed over the last few months was starting to kick in. I could almost hear Dr. Stern's even-keeled voice inside my head. It wasn't the first time an animal injured by a vehicle collision had been brought in, but I didn't know much—or anything, really—about turtles.

What I *did* know was that it was in really bad shape. And this didn't look like an ordinary pet turtle sold in stores, either. It had unique, swirly yellow-and-brown markings all over its shell and body. It looked like a beautiful marble, nothing I'd ever seen before, even at pet stores and the zoo. This turtle could've been an endangered species, for all I knew.

"This is a small-animal practice," I said as despair set in. I knew Dr. Stern was a skilled veterinarian, but reptiles weren't her specialty. The clinic was understaffed, I knew, because Miss Janice was usually complaining about how much work she had to do, and Dr. Stern was planning on hiring a second vet tech but just hadn't found the right candidate yet. "You need, like, a *wildlife* clinic," I said to the girl. "I'm not sure we can help. Its injuries look pretty bad. I'm not even sure it's alive."

I squinted, trying to examine the turtle as closely as possible without touching it. Its eyes were open, revealing bright red pupils. Did that mean it was dead, the red eyes? Was that blood? I didn't even know what vital signs to look for. Do turtles blink? Do their shells expand and contract when they take a breath? It certainly wasn't moving or making any noise. I felt helpless.

"But you guys were on Google Maps," the girl countered. "The *nearest vet's office*. I asked Siri. You have a FIVE-STAR RATING! C'mon—you have to do something! Where's the doctor?" She looked as frantic as I felt inside, and I began to wonder whether maybe she really did run over the turtle but didn't want to admit it, and whether she was flustered about saving the turtle's life or about running late for wherever she had to be or about getting a parking ticket and having to pay a fine.

"Dr. Stern is with a patient under anesthesia in a sterile operating room," I said, glancing up at the clock. The surgery started about thirty minutes ago, and I wasn't sure how long they'd be in there. Sometimes Dr. Stern took longer on things because she was teaching Daniel steps along the way. I stared at the dark red bloodstains on the blanket, trying to decide what to do.

The second hand on the clock continued to tick.

We were running out of time.

"You know about this stuff, right? I mean—you're *here*, aren't you?" The girl raised a perfectly penciled eyebrow. "You must know what to Google at least. . . ."

"What, you think I'm going to tape its shell back together? This turtle needs more than Google!" I said, exasperated. "I'll be right back. Wait here."

I gently lifted up the blanket-wrapped turtle and carried it down the hallway toward the surgery room. I didn't have free hands to knock, so I just thumped at the closed door with the top of my head until finally the door cracked open and Daniel's head poked through.

"Josie, this isn't the time to interrupt us. I hope you have a good reason," he said, a pinched expression on his face. I narrowed my eyes. I had never interrupted them in surgery before. *Of course* I had a good reason!

"It's an emergency. Injured turtle."

Daniel looked down at my arms. I could see on his face that he was piecing the story together. He swung open the door and called out to Dr. Stern.

"Josie's here—animal emergency."

"Josie? What's going on?" Dr. Stern's voice was muffled a little from behind her blue face mask, but there was no irritation in her voice, just a mix of kindness and concern. She was hunched over the small dog on the operating table and had a silvery instrument of some kind in her right hand.

I held back tears, not wanting to explain again why I was holding a wild turtle with bleeding eyes and a broken shell. I could barely even look at the poor creature without my chin starting to tremble.

"Turtle. Eleven-inch-long carapace, cracked in several places," Daniel jumped in. I wasn't sure whether to be grateful or annoyed. "Likely an automotive injury. Is that correct, Josie?"

I nodded. "Driver's in the lobby." It wasn't the time to go into details.

Dr. Stern jutted her chin toward Daniel but continued to work on the dog. "Tell me what you see," she instructed. "I'm scrubbed in. I can't come over there."

He leaned down, peering carefully at the turtle. "First crack is near the top."

"Where?"

"Um—over the thorax."

251

"Okay." She paused. My nerves were electric, and it felt like the whole room was moving in slow motion. "Is the heart visible?"

"Not from this angle, no. But the top crack is extensive." Daniel met my eyes and explained in a whisper, "Turtles have a three-chambered heart, not four, like mammals, and it's located right behind here." He pointed toward one of the cracks on its shell without touching the animal. "Look—the turtle's shell is attached to its body. Right under here are its ribs."

Usually at the clinic, Daniel spoke down to me, like he was this almighty know-it-all and I was just some kid who knew nothing, and it made my blood boil. But right now, I appreciated that he was taking the time to explain this to me. He was actually being *nice*.

"Tell me about the lungs," continued Dr. Stern, more urgent now.

"Likely crushed," said Daniel. I looked down at the yellow and brown turtle and felt like the breath was sucked right out of me, too. "Lots of blood, too."

"Species?"

"I think . . ." He tilted his head in thought. "Woodland box, maybe? Male. It's got the signature red eyes. I used to see them on campus sometimes. They're pretty common."

"Alive?"

Dr. Stern's voice was calm and even, but there was a hint of something else, a tone I had just started to learn over the summer. That's when I realized it. She wasn't quizzing Daniel about the turtle's injuries because she had hope for its survival. . . . No.

She was *teaching* him.

I looked at Daniel and watched his face soften into a look that I instantly recognized.

"No," he said. "It's dead."

Suddenly the turtle felt heavier in my hands, like I was holding a giant brick and not a poor little squished reptile that was about to be bandaged up and rehabilitated. I had never held a dead animal before. I hadn't even *seen* a dead animal before, unless you counted Amelia's goldfish over the years, and when Ralphie, Mrs. Taglioni's old sugar glider, had died last winter and I watched Dr. Stern put it in her black medical bag. But that was like a dark blur, and for only a second.

"Set the turtle in the sink, Josie," said Dr. Stern. "We'll dispose of it."

I blinked back my confusion. "The sink?"

"Yes, the deep sink. Along the wall." She looked up at me from the other side of the unconscious dog. "Thank you."

I didn't move. "But . . . aren't we going to bury it?"

Daniel coughed into a closed fist. I felt my face redden.

"Is it someone's pet, Josie?" Dr. Stern asked, offering me a kind smile.

I shook my head. "No."

"Roadkill," said Daniel in a matter-of-fact tone.

I narrowed my eyes at him. Roadkill or not, it wasn't a very kind thing to say about an innocent little animal.

"Josie," Dr. Stern said, "if it's a common, wild creature, we're going to use this opportunity to learn something, so the turtle's death is not wasted. We're going to dissect it," she explained matter-of-factly.

I looked down at the dead turtle again. Flashes passed through my mind of its shell being torn off with those long, silvery surgery instruments. Daniel looking at its ribs along the underside. Dr. Stern pointing at its organs and telling him to take notes on turtle anatomy. Suddenly, I became more aware of the metallic smell of blood in the air, and being so close to death made my stomach turn.

My dog is dying.

Sugar. Sugar. Sugar.

I couldn't imagine her being lifeless like this. No. I wasn't ready to say good-bye to her.

"Oh" is all I said in response, because I didn't want to say more and risk throwing up.

I walked over to the sink and gently set the turtle inside, being careful not to touch it or look in its sad, dead, red eyes. I stood there for a moment, unsure if I should rip the dirty blanket out from underneath it to return to the girl, until finally deciding to just leave it there.

"Um. Hope the surgery is going well," I said, moving toward the door.

"Josie?" Dr. Stern looked up again. I stopped in my tracks, my sneakers squeaking on the tile floors, like they do in gym class. "You okay?"

No.

I wish I could call Lucy right now.

"Yep." I nodded. "I—I'm going to go home now."

She smiled. "Of course. Thank you, as always, for spending time with us. And for trying to help the turtle."

I gently closed the door behind me, trying to figure out how I'd break the news to the driver. What would she say? Threaten to give us a one-star rating online? As I emerged from the hallway into the clinic lobby, I started, "I'm sorry, but—" and then realized I was alone in the lobby.

She'd left.

Just like that.

I couldn't stand people sometimes.

Chapter 19

THE LAST GOODBYE

Saturday came with clear morning skies and a flood of bright sunshine. It was the kind of summer day that us kids dream about, when you can run barefoot through the grass and feel a soft breeze through your hair and laugh with your friends while fireflies spark in the darkening sky.

The whole family drove out to Mr. Upton's farm in the van. Mrs. Taglioni was back at her townhouse today, finishing up the packing with her movers. We even brought the seven adorable puppies on the trip—in their crate of course, to keep them secure in the car. I'd only *barely* convinced Dad to trust me with all the animals. Reminding him that I only had one week left with them did the trick.

Sugar slept most of the drive, but by the time we got to Mr. Upton's farm, she had popped up on all fours in the far back, trying to keep her balance, nose lifted toward the new scents that filtered in through the rolled-down windows.

"Thatta girl!" said Tom, patting her on the head. "There's that energy I like to see in my dog."

Ellen rolled her eyes. "Your dog?"

My brother grinned his classic toothy grin. "And I'm really looking forward to seeing my pig."

"*Your* pig!" I play-smacked his shoulder. "Very funny."

"Hey, I found it! And named it."

"*Her*," Amelia and I said at the same time.

"She's technically Mr. Upton's pig now," piped up Sarah from the middle seat. As we turned down the long driveway, she added, "Can we ride the horses, Josie?"

"Not today, but Mr. Upton said that sometime when his kids are visiting they can help teach us how to ride. He has a neighbor come over sometimes to exercise the horses, too, I think?"

Sarah leaned back into her seat and stared out the window. "So. Cool."

I gave my family a quick recap on the status of the

animals at the farm, and for a brief second, I felt like how I imagined Mr. Upton might feel when he picked up Lucy and Mrs. Taglioni and me from the train station. It felt good to be on the flip side of the conversation, and Amelia giggled when I told her about Chip the chipmunk, and how Pogo the donkey really loved carrots, and that Hamlet took long naps in the shade after catching Frisbees.

"Oh, Hammie!" my little sister squealed as Mom parked the van in the driveway. "I can't wait to see her— it's been sooooooo long!"

We all got out of the van. Tom helped me lift Sugar so she wouldn't have to jump down, and we gently placed her on the ground. "You okay, Sugar?" I asked her, and she moved slowly toward the freshly cut, green grass, nose pressed to the blades. I leashed up each puppy as I pulled them out of the crate, and I let Amelia race around with Speedy on the pinky-promise condition that she would not let her out of her sight.

Mr. Upton waved from the front porch. He had a navy apron tied around his waist, and he was clutching a spatula in one hand. "Just grilling burgers out back," he called out to us. "C'mon up when you're hungry! Josie, give them the farm tour, if you like! Oh, all the dogs are here, too! How wonderful. Let 'em sniff around, get a feel for things."

"Hi there, Mike!" Dad called back, waving. Then he turned to us. "Hm, maybe I should go give him a hand. A family of seven is a lot to cook for." He stuck his hands in his jeans pockets and squinted in the sunlight. But it was the grin that lit up his face. I smiled, too. It was good to see Dad relaxed.

"Will do, Mr. Upton!" I yelled into my cupped hands. Then I turned to Dad. "We'll be in the barn with Hamlet. C'mon, guys!"

"Race ya!" shouted Amelia, and she bolted toward the barn, making me laugh as I tried to keep up with her and grip the puppies' leashes as they raced alongside us.

"The farm looks so different here in the summertime," said Ellen, looking around. "It's so pretty and green."

I pointed to a bucket. "Here—take a carrot, everybody."

"Oh yeah, I've got this," said Sarah. I laughed. She probably knew more about horses than I did. She showed my siblings how to properly feed the donkey and horses, with your palm flat and fingers pressed together so the animal doesn't accidentally slurp up a finger. Then I motioned toward the beautiful cursive sign above Hamlet's pen and explained that Carlos had painted it.

"Guys, isn't Hamlet massive?" I said as we approached the far part of the barn.

"Whoa!"

"No way!"

"HAMMIE!"

"She's *huge*!"

"Oh my, Hamlet, you sure have grown! Still as sweet as ever, though . . . ," said Mom. "Oh look! Ha. Stephen's old slippers."

Our big, pink pig was dirty as ever, too. She wiggled and wriggled right along the wooden gate, and I opened it up wide, letting her out.

"Are you sure she can roam around the property, Josie?" Mom looked concerned. "She won't run off?"

"Well, when it's just me and Lucy, we use a leash— Hamlet's still fast, even though she's gotten real big and lazy over the summer. But since there's so many of us today, I think she'll stick around. I want to show you guys her tricks!"

"Now *that's* what I'm talking about," Tom said,

reaching for the Frisbee balanced on a nearby shelf. "Ready, Millie?"

"Yep!" Amelia grinned. "Aww, look! Sugar's sniffing Hammie!"

Sugar had been exploring the barn for the last few minutes, but it was true: now that Hamlet was loose and nearby, she'd taken a renewed interest in our farm pig.

They sniffed each other from all sides. Sugar's tail wagged and thumped against Sarah's leg. I clutched my hand around a barn post, barely breathing. After they were satisfied with examining each other's scents, Sugar licked Hamlet's snout. The pig oinked, as if to say, *Well, there you are!*, making my heart swell with happiness.

As we walked outside to the grassy field, and into the scent of charcoal on the grill and wildflowers, my steps felt lighter. Amelia and Tom played Frisbee with Hamlet, while Sarah sat on the wooden fence petting one of the horses, and Sugar lay down for another nap. Mom and Ellen laughed as Tom and Amelia did sprints, back and forth, back and forth, and a patch of yellow dandelions distracted Hamlet.

We spent the afternoon eating hamburgers on picnic tables behind the house, and even Sugar ate part of a super-juicy hamburger patty. She seemed to be in good spirits today, with her eyes half closing as every breeze swept over the farm, enjoying the sunshine and new aromas and extra-special treats.

"She seems happy," Mom said, watching Sugar at her feet. I took a bite of potato salad and swung my feet off the picnic bench. "Great idea to bring her, Josie."

"Yeah," I said, smiling. "She does. And calm."

"*I'm* happy, too!" added Amelia, her mouth full of cheeseburger. A string of cheddar cheese dripped down her chin, making Tom laugh.

"I'm glad, honey," said Dad from across the table. "I'm happy, three."

Mr. Upton updated my family on Mrs. Taglioni's moving date—which was only *four* days away, I could barely believe it—and how he was taking some new medications that seemed to help the inflammation in his knee.

"It's been great having Lucy and Josie come visit every month," Mr. Upton said. "We love having visitors at the farm. You all are welcome anytime you'd like to escape the city."

"Thanks, Mike," Dad said. "We appreciate that."

"I want to escape the city *all* the time," deadpanned Sarah.

I grinned again. More farm escapes sounded great to me, too.

"And thanks again for letting us bring out Sugar and the puppies," added Mom. "Our sweet dog is in her final days, and it's wonderful to see her in such good spirits today."

Mr. Upton nodded, appearing to search for the right words. "I understand how dogs are like our family members," he said. "I lost a dog once. . . . It's a hard thing to endure."

Ellen said, "You had a dog?"

He nodded. "Oxen was his name. St. Bernard mix. He passed away many years ago, at only eight years old. Such a loyal, loving dog. Truly my best friend. . . ."

"I'm so sorry," said Sarah. "Eight is really young for a dog."

I glanced at my sister. Overall, she'd been unusually quiet today. Maybe she was processing everything about Sugar's health, too. From helping Dr. Stern at the veterinary clinic, I'd learned that animal owners handled grief in different ways. Some pet owners were outspoken in the face of bad news, while others stuffed their feelings inside. It seemed like Sarah was guarding her feelings today, and it made me worry about her.

"Yes," Mr. Upton agreed. "Eight is too young. Unfortunately, that's how it goes with big dogs. They don't live as long as some other breeds. . . ."

"Sugar is twelve!" said Amelia. "She's ancient!"

Mr. Upton raised a spoonful of potato salad to his mouth and added, "Well, then I'm glad Sugar was able to come today, too. I'm sorry to hear that she's not doing well. It's real painful when our pets grow old. . . ."

"Yeah." Dad's voice broke, and I noticed he fed Sugar a piece of hamburger under the table. I felt tears sting my eyes, but I tried to blink them back. I didn't want to feel sad today. Today was supposed to be an uplifting day for our family, and for Sugar. I needed to stay positive.

"If you like dogs so much, maybe you should adopt a puppy, Mr. Upton!" said Amelia, her eyebrows rising in excitement. "Josie and her friends are throwing a puppy Adoptathon next Saturday! If you don't hurry, they're all going to get new homes, and you'll miss your chance! That would be a real bummer. See how cute they are?" She motioned to them snoozing, playing, and nibbling on grass near my mom.

"Hmmm." Mr. Upton rubbed his chin.

My sister nodded. "You'd be a good dog owner, even though it's been a long time. I can tell. All the animals seem to like you. Even Sugar."

"Sugar likes everybody, Millie," I said with a smile. "But I agree. You should think about it, Mr. Upton."

He threw his hands into the air, grinning, like we were cornering him with a topic he hadn't been prepared to discuss. We ate until our bellies were stuffed and the high afternoon sun had begun to slowly drop toward the horizon. As the sky took on an orange-pink hue, Mr. Upton got his guitar from the house and asked us, "Anyone up for a little sunset campfire and some s'mores?"

"Ahhh, s'mores! All *right*, Mr. Upton! And I'll help with the fire," said Tom.

My brother and Ellen ventured off to gather sticks and firewood while everyone else fell into conversation about Ellen's online class. Amelia kicked around a soccer ball, and Sarah snapped photos and shot videos of the horses on her cell phone. Mom got the crate from the car, placed it in the shade near my dad, and secured all the puppies inside for a good nap.

I drew in a long, deep breath and listened, letting all the farm sounds reach my ears in their own rhythm and time.

Crickets hummed around us.

A breeze rustled through the tall oak trees' leaves.

My little sister laughed as Sarah tried to get the soccer ball from her. The puppies yipped for more tiny bites of burger.

The farm was so beautiful, it helped lift all the worries inside me, even if just for a short while. The scent of grass filled my nose, and I could still taste the tang of ketchup in my mouth. Then, in the branches of a nearby tree, I spotted the instantly recognizable black-and-white feathers of a city bird.

It felt like a lightning bolt had struck my spine. I sat up straighter, squinting, trying to zoom my vision as if my eyes were camera lenses.

I was right. There it was, not far off from where we were sitting.

A tuxedo pigeon.

"Wow," I whispered. This was only the third time that I'd seen one in my whole life. At least, in its tuxedo suit. Legend has it that these magical birds normally disguise themselves as regular old pigeons, but when they're on a special mission, their feathers transform into the signature black-and-white pattern of a fancy tuxedo.

The last time I'd seen one had been on this very farm, many months ago—the day that we gave Hamlet to Mr. Upton.

Did the tuxedo pigeon live here?

A tightening clutched my heart.

Or was it on a mission, right now, in this very moment?

I didn't know why, but the strangest sensation flooded through me.

What if its mission had to do with Sugar?

I stood up from the picnic bench and spun around and around again. I desperately searched the property for our dog's golden-blond fur and the whisk of a long, fluffy tail. My family had all retreated to the fire pit area, and Mr. Upton's guitar playing carried across the farm with the delicious scent of toasted marshmallows.

I finally spotted Sugar, a 100 yard dash away, stretched out on the grass in a patch of grass beneath the oak tree, high up on the hill overlooking the big, white house and red barn.

I broke into a run across the grass.

I pumped my arms.

I could barely breathe.

I prayed and wished and hoped so deep.

When I reached Sugar's side, her mouth flopped open as she panted softly in the cool grass. She was breathing slowly, faintly, and peacefully. A bird chirped in short bursts overhead, while another trilled a lovely melody, maybe answering a question in song.

"I'm here, girl," I whispered to Sugar, feeling tears spring to my eyes. "All your pack is right here on the farm. Don't you worry about anything. We're here. I'm here."

The smell of grilled hamburgers still clung to her fur. I reached into the pocket of my jean shorts, pulling out a whole stick of beef jerky and laying it beside her mouth. She didn't eat it, but she gave it a sniff, and I could swear a drooly doggie smile crossed her lips as she licked my hand.

Oink, oink.

I looked up. I'd forgotten that Hamlet was still wandering around the property. The pig wedged her warm, hefty body on the other side of our golden retriever. Hamlet continued to oink softly, and I patted her back to let her know that we were happy she was here. After all, Hamlet was part of our pack, too.

I wrapped my arms around Sugar. Her breathing had become more labored, and I could sense how tired she felt inside. I whispered into her droopy ears, "We all love you, Sugar. Thank you for being the best dog in the world. We love you. You can be at peace now. We love you."

She blinked her eyes and soon let them close.

The three of us just listened and smelled and breathed. I don't know how long we lay there in the soft, cool grass. It could've been ten minutes, or thirty. It didn't matter. I would've stayed there forever.

I told Sugar I loved her a million times, with my words, my energy, my heart, my tears.

Wind shook through the leaves overhead like a crackling, gentle wind chime. Hamlet softly snored. I listened to old Sugar fall into a deep, quiet sleep, and I knew in my heart what was coming next even before it happened.

Beneath that oak tree on a perfect summer day, Sugar exhaled her last breath and her heart stopped beating. I whispered my final goodbye to her with my arms wrapped around her body, and my tears moistening her soft and protective golden fur, the only other words I had left to give.

Chapter 20

IN LOVING MEMORY

We buried Sugar that evening high up on a grassy hill on Mr. Upton's farm, right next to his dog that had passed away so many years ago. It seemed right. Not just right, but perfect, with the far crackle and pop of a fizzling campfire and Mr. Upton's soft and calm words leading the service, asking us to share our memories of our special dog.

Mom recounted the story of how Sugar came to the family. Tom, with his big softy heart that he sometimes masks with jokes, broke down crying first. Dad confessed that he'd been the one to start feeding Sugar table scraps all those years ago, and that's how she became such a food beggar, and Amelia wailed, *"I'll miss brushing my feet on her fur under the table!"*

Before long, my family sat down on the cool grass and held puppies in our arms, as we if all needed to hold a heartbeat close. It felt good to cry and listen and feel the love that radiated between the members of my family. As miserable as I was inside, I also felt relieved that Sugar wasn't in pain anymore, and that I'd been right next to her in her final moments. I knew how peaceful her death was. I'd been able to tell Sugar everything in my heart, and I knew she could feel it. Our hearts were connected.

Late that night, when the summer sky turned black and stars peppered the sky, we drove back to the city in near silence, one body short and our eyes red from crying so hard. I clutched Sugar's worn brown leather collar in my hand, and each time the van hit a bump in the road, her chipped blue ID tags clinked together in my hand, another painful reminder that our old dog was gone forever.

"I'm going to miss her so much," cried Amelia, and Sarah reached across the seat and wrapped her arms around her.

"Me too," said Sarah. "Me too."

I stared out the window, marveling at how each star seemed to glow brighter out here in the countryside. I'd left my heart once before at Mr. Upton's farm, back when we gave him Hamlet, and it hurt to do it again. And this time, there was a powerful sense of finality, knowing that I'd never see Sugar again.

My heart would probably ache for a long time. That's what happens when you love a pet with that deep, true kind of love.

On Monday morning, even though she was probably still mad at me, I called Lucy anyway. I cried on the phone, telling her everything that had happened over the weekend. "It's so weird," I sobbed. "It's like sometimes I can hear her nails going *click click click* on the wooden floorboards. And whenever I pour myself a glass of water, I think about filling up her water bowl, too. Last night, my dad started bawling as he swept up her dog hair for the final time, even though he always used to complain about her shedding. Mom told him not to wipe down the back windows, because Sugar's nose print is still on one of them. She said she couldn't bear to erase it."

"I'm sorry, Josie," Lucy said. "I'm so, so sorry." And I knew she truly was.

"I don't think my family will ever recover from this," I said, wiping my eyes. "Everyone is just so sad."

"Time will help," Lucy assured me. "You guys are grieving right now. That's okay, you know?"

"Yeah." I swallowed hard. "I know. I just miss her so much."

The doorbell rang downstairs, and I heard Mom's voice carry upstairs.

"Josie?"

"I gotta go," I said into the phone. "Mom's calling me."

"Okay."

"I'm—I'm sorry, Lucy," I continued. "For everything. Lately I just feel like . . . I feel like I've been losing you, or something? And it's made me act, I don't know . . . not like myself."

"You're not losing me," Lucy said. "*I'm* losing *you*. It feels like you're too busy for me sometimes. You have all these other things going on—"

"Are you kidding?" I broke in, surprised. "I feel like you're too busy for *me*! You've got gymnastics, and SyncSong, and new friends. I know I chose to leave gymnastics, but I really miss it sometimes."

"I miss *you*!"

I sighed. "I promise I'll never be too busy for you, Luce. I want to be best friends no matter what we're into, or who we hang out with."

"Me too," she said, and I could hear her words catch in her throat. "No matter what. I'm going to my gran's, but I'll be back later." Lucy's hand covered the mouthpiece as she called out, "COMING!" and then she was back to me. "Gotta run. Dad's calling me, too. Be strong, Josie, okay? You'll feel better soon."

"Okay. I'll try. Oh! And I think the twins might pick a puppy today. They want to choose theirs before the Adoptathon."

"Oh, YAY! Keep me posted. And Josie?"

I paused, clutching the receiver at the tone change in my best friend's voice. "Yeah?"

"I'm really so sorry about Sugar. She was an awesome dog."

It felt like her words hugged my heart. "Yeah. She was. Thanks."

"Bye."

Downstairs, Dr. Stern and Lou were at the door. "I figured you wouldn't be at the clinic this morning when we opened up," said Dr. Stern. "So we wanted to pop over before my appointments and give this to your family. . . ."

Lou held something wrapped in orange tissue, and

Amelia was squirming to open it up.

"Mom wouldn't let me open this without you," my sister said.

I attempted a smile and said, "Thanks, Dr. Stern, Lou. Okay, Millie, I'm here. Open it up!"

Amelia tore open the tissue, revealing a smooth, gray cement rock. "What's this?" she asked, and then turned it over. On the back of the rock was a paw print, and etched into the cement it read, *Sugar, 2006–2018.* "Wow—look, Josie!"

"Ohhhh," I breathed, taking it from my sister. The rock was heavy in my hands. As I traced my fingers over the paw print, I could almost feel energy radiating from it, as if memories had their own heartbeats. I looked up at Dr. Stern, my vision turning blurry. "It's amazing. But . . . how did you . . . ?"

"Miss Janice molded Sugar's paw print the other day at our office. We thought that it'd be a nice way to remember how special she was, when the time came." Dr. Stern smiled warmly. "We're so sorry for your loss."

"Thank you so much for this," Mom said. "What a lovely gift. Josie, why don't you put it up on the mantel above the fireplace?"

I nodded. The rock needed to be somewhere where

we could see Sugar's paw print and remember how much we loved the only family dog we'd ever had. I carefully propped it up next to Tom's championship football trophy, Ellen's OSU acceptance letter, and the framed newspaper article about Hamlet and our family. I stepped back, looking the mantel over.

We were just missing one important thing.

"Be right back," I told everyone in the foyer as I zipped upstairs. I reached underneath my pillow on the top bunk and retrieved Sugar's old brown leather collar that I'd slept with last night. It wasn't fair to keep it to myself. The whole family loved her, too. I went back downstairs and added it to our collection of special objects on the mantel, then stepped back again, smiling.

"Thanks, Dr. Stern," I said. "That really means a lot."

"I've also come with good news," Dr. Stern said. "Mr. Johnson and his girlfriend would like to adopt a puppy! You mentioned that Houdini might be a good fit for them?"

I grinned. "Definitely! Houdini's got loads of energy, so he's going to need an owner who'll take him on runs and play with him a lot. Plus, Gruff seems really active. I think Gruff and Houdini would have a lot of fun wrestling together."

"Well, Mr. Johnson wants to swing by Eastside now and see if it's a good match. Would you like to be there?"

I felt my face light up. "Absolutely! And the twins want to pick out their puppy today, too."

"Two pups down, five more to go!" said Amelia, and Lou crossed his arms over his chest.

"Wish *we* could keep one," Lou grumbled.

"Me too," Amelia sighed. "But you have like a million animals come to the veterinary clinic that you can visit anytime, so that counts for something!" Then she added, "C'mon! Let's play catch in the back. And I want to hear about camp! You've been gone FOR-EV-ERRRR!"

They bolted to the back door with Mom laughing and calling out, *"NO RUNNING IN THE HOUSE!"* to distracted ears. She and Dr. Stern made eye contact and they both shook their heads, as if they shared an unspoken parenting language.

"Mom, is that okay, if I go over to Eastside now with Dr. Stern and Houdini?"

"Sure, sweetie. Just call me soon, okay?"

"Okay!" I bit my lip. "Dr. Stern—can you wait just one moment please? I need to find paper and a pen real quick. . . ."

On the walk to the veterinary clinic, I hooked the

pink bike chain around the Three Stoops, and tucked in my handwritten note, which read *Let's plan Dog Days Adoptathon details! FIVE DAYS TO GO!*

Hope surged inside my body. We could get all these puppies adopted into homes—I knew we could. First the puppies lost their real mama and now Sugar, who had kept a watchful eye over them in our house.

These puppies needed forever families, and needed them soon.

I wouldn't let them down.

Chapter 21

DOG DAYS

The puppy Adoptathon was the chatter of the whole block. The next few days were a whirlwind of preparation, but finally, the big day arrived. We were as ready as we could be. Dr. Stern gave the puppies the health stamp of approval, and for just fifty bucks a pup, each dog came with a red leash, a collar, a harness, and a few days' supply of puppy food.

It was a beautiful day, so in front of our townhouse, the Three Stoops crew assembled portable fencing that had been in a storage closet inside the veterinary clinic. This way, the puppies could play freely and safely while people made their decisions.

Carlos had made posters that read, ADOPT, DON'T SHOP! with photos and details and hung them all around the neighborhood. Fernanda and Lucy printed out the individual puppy profiles from the website Fernanda had made, and we kept them in a big stack on a table with adoption applications and Dr. Stern's business cards.

I even called Evette Waters, the reporter I knew from the cable station. She'd been the one who had helped get the word out about Hamlet—and she gave us a shout-out on the morning news, too! My siblings shared event graphics on social media, and my parents posted the digital event flier on the neighborhood Facebook page. Our event had great buzz already!

"C'mon, Carlos," Fernanda said, putting her hands on her hips. "We've got to pick our puppy before they all get adopted out!"

"But I'm so confused," said Carlos, shaking his head. "I like them all. But I still like Tugger the best."

"Mom said we have to agree, or it's a no-go."

Carlos turned to me. "Which one would you adopt?"

My hands turned clammy. "Lucky," I told them honestly, even though I knew that part of me would still be jealous if my next-door neighbors adopted my favorite puppy of the whole litter. But at least it'd mean that I'd get to see her all the time.

"Why don't you adopt her?" suggested Fernanda. Then, more gently, "Now that you don't have a dog, you know? Maybe your parents would be okay with it."

I bit my lip, thinking through what Mr. Upton said the other day, about how his dog died many years ago. He still wasn't ready to move on. I wasn't sure when I'd be ready, either. Do you *ever* get over your dog dying? Sugar was a part of me, and a part of our family. I didn't want to betray her by getting a new dog too fast. That'd be like forgetting her . . . or trying to forget her.

I still had a lot of grieving to do.

"Maybe one day," I said, blinking back tears.

"If you wait too long, Lucky will get adopted by someone else," Carlos warned.

I nodded. "Yeah. I know. But finding the right homes for all the puppies is what's most important."

"I still vote we pick Babbles," said Fernanda, flashing her brother an accusing look. "She's so fun. Just *look* at her!"

In the secured play area, Babbles wrestled with Speedy. It was speed versus strength, and Carlos laughed as Babbles pawed at Speedy's neck, trying to pin him on the grass.

"I have an idea," I broke in. "Let's position Tugger

and Babbles next to each other in the play zone and ask the dogs what they want to do."

"I think it's a good idea," said Grace, suddenly appearing next to me. I shuffled my feet, unsure of what to say. I hadn't seen her since our awkward Vans situation. But Grace found words when I couldn't. Maybe that's what happens when you're thirteen. "Josie . . . can I talk to you for a second?"

I nodded. "BRB, guys," I said to the twins, following Grace to the brick steps nearby.

"I . . ." Grace paused, sighing. "I wanted to say that I'm sorry, Josie. I know it wasn't your fault about the shoe thing. And . . . I was rude." Her shoulders began to shake, like she was trying to hide how nervous she was. "I've never moved before, and I didn't want to come here. And it seemed like you guys were all such close friends and I was sort of intruding in your group. When Lucy told me that you would be really upset that your neighbor was moving away . . . I just . . . well, I felt like maybe you'd hate me for it. So that made it easier to pretend not to like you."

My tense muscles relaxed. "I'm sorry, too, Grace," I said honestly. "And I *am* glad you're here. I think you'll like the city if you give it a chance. We might not have the ocean, but it's still pretty cool. Truce?"

She grinned. "Truce."

We hugged and I said, "Wait right here!" and zipped inside my townhouse. When I came back a minute later, I swung her washed and dried Vans by the shoelaces and handed them to her gently. "All clean!" I said. But then I gestured to the puppy Adopathon down the street, laughing, "Although I can't promise they'll stay clean long."

Grace laughed. "You know, I actually wish we could keep a puppy. We're going to be doing major renovations though, so I bet my parents would say no."

"Well, the twins are about to pick one. Want to watch?"

"Sure!"

We walked back to the little outdoor playpen, where Tugger and Babbles now pawed at each other. Fernanda said, "Whichever puppy reveals itself as our puppy is final, okay, Los? No negotiating or changing minds. Deal?"

Grace raised an eyebrow. "Reveals itself?"

"I don't know." Fernanda sighed, exasperated. "Josie said to ask the puppies what they wanted. My brother isn't making this any easier, so I'll try anything at this point! Deal, Carlos?"

"Yep. Deal."

The twins shook hands. It was go time!

We watched the two puppies wrestle, yelp, nibble on each other's ears, play-bite, and box with their paws.

"They're both sooooo cute," cooed Lucy, appearing beside me with a lollipop in her hand. "You really can't go wrong with either one."

"What have we here?" said a male voice behind us, and we all spun around.

"Hey, Dad!" Grace said in surprise. "Guys, this is my dad. Well, one of them. Dad, these are the new neighbors I was telling you about. . . ."

He grinned. "Nice to meet you all. We're looking forward to moving into the neighborhood."

Grace rolled her eyes and said, "Me too. Living out of a suitcase is the worst."

"I'm Josie," I said. "I live right next door. It's nice to meet you. We love Mrs. Taglioni, but she's going to an awesome farm, and it'll be nice having Grace next door."

Grace smiled, and her purple eye shadow glittered like diamond dust in the sunlight. "Dad, what're you doing here?"

"What do you think I'm doing here?" He pulled a pen from his shirt pocket and held it in the air. "Filling out an adoption application, of course!"

"*No way!*" Grace jumped up and down. "Seriously?!"

"Seriously." He laughed. "As long as you'll help with taking care of it. But since I'll be working from home, I thought it'd be nice to have an excuse to get outside for a nice, long walk. I can't sit in front of the computer all day, can I? And I know how hard this move has been for you, Grace. I think a new addition to the family is just what we need."

Grace's eyes lit up as she searched the puppy pen and looked at the twins. "I might have an idea. . . ."

"What if . . ." Fernanda grinned.

". . . we *each* adopt one of them?" Grace finished.

"You can have Tugger!" Carlos broke in, and we burst out laughing, making Carlos smile his rare full-braces smile.

"Deal." Grace shook his hand, and Carlos grinned a little bigger, if that was even possible. I couldn't help but laugh. I'd never seen Carlos act like this around a girl before. At least it wasn't just Sully and I who were so awkward around each other!

Fernanda cheered and reached down to pick up Babbles. The puppy licked her cheek. "We won, Babbles! We won!"

"You *all* won," laughed Lucy. "There are no losers

here. Now, we've gotta make sure the other puppies get good homes."

"Definitely," I agreed.

When Mr. Johnson had come into the office a few days ago, he'd loved Houdini's high energy. "I'll take him!" he had said after a test jog with the dog down the block. He'd handed me two twenties and a ten, which I'd slipped into the Adoptathon money pouch to use as change for the other adoptions.

So three puppies had been adopted into good homes now. Only four more to go!

Even my siblings helped out at the event, just like in the final days of finding Hamlet a forever home. Tom wore this cardboard sign around his neck that read DOG DAYS ADOPTATHON TODAY! with a giant arrow pointed toward our group. He danced up and down the block, trying to rally the interest of passing drivers. Normally that type of thing would be sooooo embarrassing, but today is was actually pretty funny. A few people even pulled over to see what all the excitement was about!

I overheard Daniel explaining to Ellen the process of trimming a dog's nails and how most people choose to remove a dog's dewclaws. Sully's sister, Trish, and Sarah were in charge of the application forms, handing out clipboards and ensuring that everyone who petted the puppies used hand sanitizer beforehand.

"Awwww, how cute!" cooed a mom pushing her toddler past in a stroller. She stopped the wheels just a foot short of the baby gates, and her son, maybe two years old, excitedly chattered over the playful puppies.

I heard someone laugh next to me. When I turned, Sully had moved a little closer to me on the sidewalk. Our arms almost touched each other, and it felt like electricity was radiating off his skin and onto mine. My grin was so big, it was probably bigger than Carlos's. Maybe one of these days I'd be brave enough to reach for his hand to hold it.

By two o'clock in the afternoon, Blue and Rocky had been adopted, too. That meant only Lucky and Speedy were left.

"I can't stay much longer," Lucy told me. "Gymnastics practice starts soon. But . . . do you want to do a SyncSong with me later?"

I pressed up on my toes and grinned. "Yeah, that'd be super fun."

We said goodbye, and soon everyone started to drift away. The twins wanted to take Babbles back to their place and introduce her to their mom. Grace had to help her dads with a few last-minute things before tomorrow, and Sully had to eat a late lunch before basketball camp that afternoon at the community center.

Before he left, Sully kicked the sidewalk with his sneaker, lingering by me as if he had something important to say. A band of sweat glistened across his forehead. He blinked a few times too many before saying, "So, um, I've been hiding something from you."

My heart hammered in my chest. "Um, okay."

Sully pulled his Case File notebook from his backpack and spun it to a page. Then he exhaled loudly and turned it around, so I could read the handwritten words on the top.

The Case for Asking Josie to Be My Girlfriend, it read.

My lips parted into a smile, and I met Sully's eyes. He smiled. I looked back at the page. Every line on the page was filled with his reasons. No wonder he'd been so secretive with his notebook around me!

Josie is the smartest person I know.

Josie has the biggest heart for animals.

She makes me nervous, but like in a good way.

I knew my face had been taken over by a huge, goofy grin, but I couldn't hold it back, that's how much my heart swelled in that moment.

Sully cleared his throat. I looked up again, feeling my heart race. "Ha, I'm nervous, too," I admitted. "But . . . like in a good way."

I was rambling again, but this time I didn't care. Sully still *liked* me! I had to restrain myself from jumping up and down.

"So . . ." He shifted his weight to his other leg. "Does that mean we're going out?"

Ahh! He wanted to be my boyfriend!

"Yeah. Sure." I shrugged, as if having a longtime crush on your next-door neighbor was no big deal, when it was the absolute hugest deal ever. "We're going out."

Sully grinned so big, I thought his baseball hat might pop off his head. "Okay, cool."

"Cool."

Thump, thump.

I couldn't stop smiling. But instead of worrying about looking goofy and immature, I just let myself smile.

Maybe that's how it feels when your first crush becomes your first official boyfriend.

"Well. See ya," Sully said. He stuck his hands in his pocket.

"Yeah. See ya. Have fun at basketball!"

Should I give him a hug?

We ended up awkwardly waving goodbye to each other, which made me laugh. Okay, so maybe it would take a little while for Sully and me to be normal around each other, but this was a start.

I stood there for a moment, staring down at two of the cutest puppies I'd ever seen play inside the fenced-in area. Speedy, who was timid and fast and oh so sweet, and Lucky, with her curious nature. I wasn't going to settle for anything less than the perfect homes for these two puppies.

A cloud formed overhead, masking the stream of sunshine that we'd been enjoying all morning. I sensed a rainstorm coming and said to the puppies, "Let's get you two inside. . . ."

"You and your friends did a great job today, Josie," Mom said as she approached my side. "Just two left?"

"Not for long," I promised her, feeling a rush of adrenaline fill my body. "These two puppies are extra special, and I have a plan."

Mom's laugh lines crinkled around her eyes. "I bet you do, Josie Shilling," she said. "I bet you do."

Chapter 22

LUCKY DOG

Everyone on the block showed up for Mrs. Taglioni's last-minute going-away party. After all, she'd been a cornerstone of the neighborhood for decades. She deserved a big farewell!

The Three Stoops crew decorated Mrs. Taglioni's front stoop—well, Grace's stoop now—with twisted pink streamers and little potted flowers that Mom had picked up from an outdoor market downtown. Someone had set up a giant rectangular folding table, complete with a pink polka-dot tablecloth and a giant white-icing cake that had *Good Luck, Mrs. T!* written on it in big cursive frosting. Mom let me wear makeup and showed me some of her beauty tricks. Sarah had given me a whole bunch of her old clothes—the cute ones, too, not just ratty T-shirts—so I was even wearing a newish outfit for the big day.

Speedy and Lucky had stayed at our place the last few nights, and I'd gone over my plan with my parents to get their green light. Dad had his doubts about it all, but I told him to just wait and see, and the puppies would make the final decision.

Sometimes, when you sit quietly and let animals do the talking, you find that it's easy to know what to do. Hamlet taught me that.

"We're going to really miss you, Molly," said Dr. Stern, giving our elderly neighbor a big hug.

"Oh, thank you for everything, Cassandra. Please come visit the farm, and bring Lou, too! Amelia can introduce him to all the animals."

"That sounds lovely. We certainly will."

Over the next few hours, we all ate big squares of fluffy chocolate cake and played with the puppies on their leashes—Speedy, Lucky, Babbles, and Tugger were all in attendance—and Mrs. Taglioni hugged so many people, I lost count.

I sat on my front stoop, licking frosting off my spoon. I watched as everyone cried a mix of sad and happy tears and listened to the funny stories people shared about Mrs. Taglioni. I grinned. It must feel good to have neighbors who love you so deeply like that. And I knew that love would go with her, no matter where she moved. After all, I had grown to love Mrs. Taglioni, too.

"Hi there, Josie," said a voice, and I looked up, squinting, until Mr. Upton's smiling face blocked the sunlight.

"Oh! Hey, Mr. Upton," I said. "I'm glad you made it!"

"Well, thanks for the invite. It was fun driving the ol' truck into the city. Usually Molly comes out to visit me, not the other way around. Parking, though, is another story." He chuckled. "This seat taken?"

"Nope. All yours!" I patted the brick step. Then I lowered my voice. "Did you . . . bring what we talked about?"

He nodded, handing me a small white envelope. "This is amazing—thanks, Mr. Upton!" I said, tucking it in my pocket. I was going to save this little surprise for later.

"It's the least I can do," he said, spearing some cake with a fork and breaking off a bite. "You've been a mighty fine friend to my sister, Josie, and I thank you for that."

I beamed. "Thanks, Mr. Upton. But she's been a good friend to me, too." I set down my empty plate and leaned back on my palms, thinking. I'd been waiting for the right time to tell him my idea, and maybe now was it. "Can you wait here a second?" I asked him, and he laughed again.

"I've got a seat and my cake. I'm not going anywhere."

"Okay, good!"

I zipped inside my house and through the back door, where Amelia and Lou were tossing a rope toy with Speedy and Lucky. "Gotta take the pups," I told them, attaching leashes to their harnesses. Now that the puppies were bigger and stronger, we kept collars and harnesses on at the same time outside, so that they couldn't slip off their leashes during walks.

"Whyyyy?" whined Amelia. "We were having so much fun!"

"Sorry," I said, and then I grinned. "Trust me, okay?"

"Yeah, yeah." Then she threw Lou a mischievous smile. "Race ya to a second piece of cake!" and she bolted out the back gate and around the block, her best friend laughing and trying to keep up.

I led the puppies back to the front stoop, where Mr. Upton waited. "This one's Lucky," I reminded him, tugging her curious nose away from his frosting-smeared paper plate. Mr. Upton laughed, and I added, "She's really sweet and loves to play. One time I caught her carrying around my sneaker like a ball. She still has accidents sometimes, but she's getting better at being housebroken. And this"—I held up Speedy—"is Speedy. She was the littlest of her whole litter, but she's grown a lot since we've been fostering her. Speedy's the fastest one, so that's how she got her name! She's kinda timid and shy, but I think with the right owner, she'll come out of her shell a bit more. I think she's just used to having bigger, stronger personalities around her all the time."

"Well, I can understand that. I do have Molly as a sister," said Mr. Upton. "Wow, these are the only two you have left? It must have been a wonderful Adoptathon!"

"Yep." I nodded. "The puppies all went to really great homes. But . . . I . . . wondered if you'd given more thought to getting another dog? Like, if you were ready yet?"

Mr. Upton inhaled deeply and then reached over and picked up Speedy. He stroked her back for a moment and said, "I'm not sure. It's a hard weight to bear, losing a dog."

I nodded, my heart hurting as I thought of Sugar. "Yeah. Yeah it is."

"I don't think another dog could replace Oxen."

"I don't think another dog could replace Sugar." I

paused. "But one of these puppies is yours, if you want it, Mr. Upton. I wanted to make sure you had one last chance. They're really good and healthy dogs. If you think you might be ready, I know either one would be a loyal companion for you."

We sat there for a moment in silence, each cradling a soft, snuggly puppy and watching the farewell party continue before us. Amelia had ripped some streamers off Mrs. Taglioni's front stoop and was wearing them around her waist like a belt. Daniel had walked down from the clinic and was talking with Ellen over a can of Pepsi, which made me shake my head and smile. Tom was wearing sunglasses—I still think they were Mom's old pair—and exchanging jokes with Mr. Johnson. I spotted Dad giving Gruff and Houdini pats on the back.

I glanced at Mr. Upton. He seemed just as lost in his thoughts as me. Finally, he broke the silence. "Maybe one day I'll say the same thing about this pup."

I cocked my head sideways. "What do you mean?"

"I was thinking that, you know, all my animals have been wonderful companions in their own ways. I've had lots of donkeys and horses, and you know, Hamlet is a real special pig. I miss Oxen every day, but getting a new dog doesn't mean that I'd miss him any less. You can grieve one pet and celebrate another, just like you can make new friends without giving up your old ones. So maybe this is the right timing after all. It could be good for me and Molly to have some puppy energy around the farm, to keep us old-timers young. . . ."

"Wait, are you saying . . . ?" I could barely contain my excitement.

"I'm saying that if it'd be okay with you, I'd like to adopt this little girl puppy. Speedy, you say?"

"Yes! Speedy!" I grinned. "That's amazing, Mr. Upton! You're approved!"

"What's amazing?" asked Sarah, who was standing on the sidewalk with Trish.

"Mr. Upton's going to adopt Speedy!"

"Oh, that's so *wonderful*," Mom chimed in, walking up with Mrs. Taglioni. "Speedy is very sweet. She sure is going to love running across your property!"

Mrs. Taglioni laughed. "Well, Tootsie's going to have to get used to a *lot* of life changes this week, isn't she?"

"No use fighting change," Mr. Upton said, stroking Speedy's head. "Sometimes change is good, even when it's hard. That's the beauty of life."

"You know, I think you're right," I said, looking around at all my neighbors and family gathered on the sidewalk on a beautiful, sunny August day. A few months ago, I never would've guessed that we'd be out here, saying goodbye to Mrs. Taglioni and welcoming a new family next door, or that Sugar would have passed away and a new puppy would be in my arms.

I hugged Lucky close, letting her nuzzle against my neck until she started chewing on my hair. "Lucky!" I laughed, pulling her away.

Yeah. Change wasn't always easy, and sometimes it didn't feel good at first, but I realized your heart could heal a little, bit by bit, over time.

Sometimes you just needed a pack to teach you that.

"So, only one puppy left?" said Dad, eyebrows pulling down in concentration.

I looked up as my family gathered around our stoop. "Yep. Just Lucky."

"Aw, man! I *really* liked Speedy!" said Amelia, swirling another pink streamer through the air. "But I'm super glad you're taking her to the farm, Mr. Upton," she added quickly. "I bet you're the best dog owner. And you have the best farm in the world! Would it be okay if I come out to visit with Josie sometimes?"

"Absolutely," Mr. Upton said. "I hope you all continue your visits."

Dad stretched his arms above his head and said casually, "Well, I am sure glad I filled out my adoption application early on. Had to make sure I got first pick. After the twins, of course. So Lucky has been saved for you since the Adoptathon began."

I looked at my dad, then my mom, and jumped to my feet. "Wait, are you joking? You're joking, right? Are you saying . . . ?! ARE YOU SERIOUS RIGHT NOW?"

Mom laughed. "Very serious."

Dad threw his hands in the air, a big grin on his face. "What can I say? You named them. I got attached."

"SURPRISE!" said Mom.

"I think adopting a puppy is a great idea," chimed in Ellen. "After Hamlet and Sugar, it feels so quiet not having a pet around the house. Plus, it seems like animals really bring us together."

"Lucky's cute," said Sarah. "But we don't need a puppy to bring us together. We have Josie!"

"I'll take the puppy anyway," Tom joked, giving me one of his classic air high fives. I laughed.

"Hurray! Lucky is ours!" shouted Amelia.

Happy tears sprang to my eyes. In that one, big moment, I understood in my heart what Mr. Upton said, about it being okay to grieve one pet while celebrating another one.

"This is amazing!" I gushed. "Thank you, Mom and Dad! Thank you, thank you!"

I brushed Lucky's soft black fur with my hand and paraded her down the stoop so she could meet everyone for the first time as an official member of the Shilling family. We were Lucky's pack now, and this was her forever home. And she'd get to grow up with some of her siblings as neighbors and playmates, too!

Mrs. Taglioni hugged me and said, "I'm happy for you, child." To my surprise, she had tears in her eyes.

"I'm happy for you, too," I told her, hugging her back. "I'll miss you, but I'm excited for you and your new adventure. It's going to be great. I promise to visit all the time."

She pinched my cheek and joked, "I'll hold you to that promise."

We spent the rest of the afternoon helping Mrs. Taglioni and the moving crew pack up the van. As the hours wound down and neighbors waved goodbye and all the cake was eaten and the table folded up, my family gave Mrs. Taglioni and Mr. Upton one last farewell before they walked to Mr. Upton's pickup truck, with Speedy on a leash, bounding alongside them.

"I'm going to miss them," sighed Amelia.

"Me too," Tom said solemnly. "Me too."

Sarah gave him a knowing look. "Repetition for emphasis?"

He made a *click-click* sound out of the side of his mouth. "Exactly."

Sarah play-punched him in the ribs, and my brother bellowed out one of his deep belly laughs, which set off a chain giggling. Before we knew it, my whole family was laughing with Lucky yelping in our midst, the newest and possibly happiest voice of all.

"Sarah," I said, handing her the white envelope I'd been saving for just the right moment. "I have something for you."

She looked at me in surprise, and she pulled out the piece of paper from inside the envelope, unfolding it. "I don't understand," she said, her eyes scanning it. "A calendar?"

"Yep. It's the weekly schedule for when Mr. Upton's daughter Annie will be at the farm for the next two months, plus a train schedule. As long as you pay for your train ticket and help muck the horse stalls when you're at the farm, Annie will give you as many free riding lessons as you want."

"*Really?!*" Sarah's eyes widened in disbelief. Then she jumped up and down and gave me the biggest hug ever. "Thanks, Josie! That's so cool of you!"

"I want riding lessons," said Tom. "But on the donkey. What's its name again? Dominick?"

Ellen groaned. "No, that's your favorite Christmas song, remember?"

"That song is terrible!" Mom laughed.

"Pogo," I told my brother. "And nobody rides him. He hangs out and eats carrots."

Tom shrugged. "That's cool. I like carrots. Maybe next time you go to the farm, I'll just eat carrots with Pogo."

"And I'll visit Sugar's grave," said Ellen, her eyes glossy.

"Yeah. That'd be nice," said Dad, his voice choking up. Amelia leaned against him, giving him a sideways hug.

"C'mon kids," said Mom cheerfully. "Let's finish cleaning up this party and start teaching our new dog some tricks!"

I took in the weathered, brown townhouses stacked

side by side down on our block and the smiles on my family's faces and thought of all the neighbors I'd grown to care about. A flood of memories washed over me like warm sunshine.

We were a pack, all of us, these people, these places, no matter where we all called home and what changes might happen down the road.

I cuddled the puppy—*our* puppy—close to my chest. She licked my nose, making me laugh.

Yeah.

I sure was lucky.

ACKNOWLEDGMENTS

My sincerest thanks go out to the following individuals who helped bring *Dog Days in the City* to print:

To Alexander Slater, my rock-star agent at Trident Media Group, who is tirelessly encouraging, honest, kind, and supportive. I'm lucky to be one of your clients.

To Jocelyn Davies, my extraordinary editor for this book, for giving my stories a home and loving Josie's character as much as I do. Thank you for helping me carve this sequel out of a jumbled mound of ideas and emotions. I am forever grateful to have had the opportunity to work with you on my first two published books. It will be ruff saying goodbye as you embark on a new adventure. I will miss you pig time! And your great animal puns and emojis! (But I can't wait to read more of your books.)

To the entire HarperCollins Children's Books team, with special thanks to editor Chris Hernandez, Kate Jackson, sales, marketing, publicity, and managing editorial. I am deeply grateful for everything you do. Thank you!

To David Curtis for another stunning cover design,

and the incredibly talented illustrator Pascal Campion for the cover art. I love it so much.

To my readers, especially those who fell in love with Josie, Hamlet, the Three Stoops, and the Shillings in *The Unlikely Story of a Pig in the City*: thank you! I hope you enjoyed the sequel as much as I loved writing it.

To Michael S. Kent, DVM, DACVIM, DACVR, professor at UC Davis, for answering my questions about veterinary medicine, and Brooke Britton, DVM, and the team at BluePearl Veterinary Partners for allowing me to shadow them for the day at an NYC animal hospital.

To Redding Veterinary Hospital in Ridgefield, Connecticut, for your compassionate, loving care of Moose in his senior years, right up until his final moments. We are eternally grateful.

To my dear Write Nite ladies, SCBWI and critique group friends, Class of 2K17 authors, agent brothers and sisters, and fellow 2017 debuts, for a beautiful literary community.

To the NYC-LA based nonprofit organization Waggy-tail Rescue, for rescuing our little Boomer and the thousands of other high-risk dogs you save from urgent circumstances. It's an honor to volunteer, foster, and advocate for you and support #AdoptDontShop.

To Nat Geo Wild and Nat Geo Channel: Thank you for all the years I contributed digital content for your dog-related programming as a freelance writer. I learned so much about canine care and behavior from watching Cesar Millan on *The Dog Whisperer* and your other informative and entertaining animal shows.

To the vegan community, especially Veganuary, Esther the Wonder Pig and Derek and Steve, Alicia Silverstone and The Kind Life, Natalie Portman, and my vegan weightlifting friends, for the inspiration, awareness, and multimedia education about living a compassionate, healthy vegan lifestyle. Your efforts changed my heart and my life, and I strive to do the same for others.

To my wonderful friends Meghan Barbieri, Erika Baylor, Amanda Goetz, Adrienne Langbauer, Julie Hanson, Vicky Loh, Karina Kuhary, Lesley Graham, Ashley Cribb, Heather O'Dell, and Heidi Browne, for being my fiercest cheerleaders in my daily life.

To the incredible people who are part of the #GoldenDropSociety, Redeemer Church, and Crunch Fitness (you're the best, Angie!): thank you for fueling my life with oils, prayer, and wellness.

To Rich, for being an awesome brother and always having my back. To Renda: I miss you and the family every day and can't wait to visit Indonesia soon. To my parents: Richard and Carol, I appreciate your ongoing prayers, guidance, and love. An extra hug to all the Kendalls and extended family, too.

To Leslee: I don't know what I'd do without you (I'll probably say that in every book I write). Saying thank you will never be enough to express my gratitude for everything you've done for me over the last year, but sisters don't always need words. I know you know. But I want you to hear it often anyway——I'm deeply grateful for you. And Ben, thanks for putting up with me! I'm thankful to have you as my new brother.

To Moose: You are gone but never forgotten. I miss you every single day. Thank you for sending us the pint-sized gift of Boomer to help ease our pain a little. I'm still waiting for you to visit me in a dream. Meet me at the beach in Waves, and we'll sprint across the sand together, okay? I'd love to see you run like the old days again, if just for a moment.

To Bobby, Townes, and Lennox: you are my pack. I love you all so much.

And my deepest praises go to God, from whom all blessings flow. Thank you for allowing me this dream of being a published children's book author.

Jodi Kendall is also the author of *The Unlikely Story of a Pig in the City*. She grew up in a household of countless pets, including hamsters, ducks, dogs, rabbits, an iguana, and even a farm pig! These days, you can find Jodi typing away at home in New York City, where she's still an animal lover at heart. Visit Jodi online at www.jodikendall.com.

Love dogs?
You may also like...

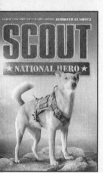

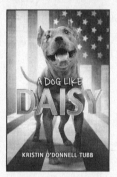

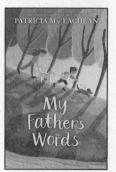